Miami SuperBowl 10

Destiny
Hope Faith
Divine

A novel by
Deaubrey Devine

To Sherrill, Thanks
for the love & support
on the novel. May God
Always bless you &
Move in your life.

Deaubrey Devine

Destiny Hope Faith Divine© by Deaubrey Devine

Published by Vision 7 Publishing©
Copyright © 2008 by Deaubrey Devine

ISBN-13:   978-0-615-21457-3
ISBN-10:   0-615-21457-6
LCCN: 2008931705

Printed in the United States of America

Cover Copyright © 2008 by Marion Designs, all rights reserved.
Cover designed by Keith Saunders
Editor: Carla M. Dean of U Can Mark My Word Editorial Services

Vision 7 Publishing
Lakeland, Fl 33815

Acknowledgements

Lord, I really appreciate you for making all of this possible for me. I'm very grateful and humble to your voice, which has spoken to me the whole time on my way to become a writer. I'm also thankful for you being my headship, covenant, and all and all throughout the rough storms and calm seas.

Mom (Diane), Dad (Curt), sisters (Curtina and Danielle), friends, family, organizations, Faithworld, and Kinard. Thank you so much for all your support and encouraging words that helped me to achieve my dream of becoming a published author. I appreciate your fellowships, conversations, meetings, and midnight talks that helped me understand the importance of life.

Venesha, thanks for birthing my blessing. It seems like it was yesterday when I emailed you for a few tips as a beginning author. I really appreciate your resources, wisdom, and taking the time out to prep me on this literary industry.

Daphine Robinson, where would I be without you? You're the heart of my knowledge and insight of my overall networks. Girl, you are truly a blessing from God. May the good Lord continue to bless you and your literary career. Please do not stop allowing God to shine through you.

LaTonya Williams, I'm thankful for you being the foundation to help me get going to the next level. Thanks for showing how to break the barrier of writing for readers and not myself while editing my manuscript. I really value your criticism and for enlightening me through your experiences that make you a bestselling author.

Editor Dean a.k.a. "Chopper Style", girl, you are the bomb! When I came to Pittsburgh and talked to you about the manuscript, I had no idea you would revamp this book to be such a smooth read. Coach, I thank you so much for the many arguments during the editing stage of this project. You really worked your magic to make this book what it is, and have blessed me with a lot of knowledge on writing a page turner.

Last but not least, I want to thank my readers. Words can't explain how you have supported me through this whole journey. I appreciate the reviews, books clubs, feedback, emails, guestbook signings, and all that you have done to support me. I honestly hope that this book will sow many seeds in your lives and give you the classic bookshelf read that you have been waiting for. You guys are awesome!

Deaubrey Devine

"Author of Real Life Situations and Issues"

<u>Dedications</u>

This book is dedicated to DJ, Camaria, and Malik. I love you with all my heart. Keep God first, make good grades, and stay focused to achieve everything your heart desires and wishes. Never let anyone tell you that you can't!

Destiny Hope Faith Divine

A novel by
Deaubrey Devine

Vision 7 Publishing
WWW.DEAUBREYDEVINE.COM

A Focused Until Completed Company

CHAPTER 1

"Cuz, I'm sure glad you invited me to come on this trip to the Bahamas. I sure needed a vacation," said Divine.

"Anytime. Danny Boy didn't want to take his wife because he said he was sending her on a vacation soon, and you know how my brother is about spending more money than he has to. Even though the trip was already paid for, he was worried about having to shell out money for incidentals, such as drinks, food, entertainment. So, he passed the tickets off to me, and I didn't want to come by myself. The tickets were actually a gift from my mom and dad, prizes they received at the annual company Christmas party. Thanks for taking off work to come," responded Cherish.

"You're welcome," replied Divine.

Cling...Cling...Cling!

"Woo! Yeah, baby, show me that big money!" shouted Cherish upon hitting the jackpot on the slot machine. The lights flashed and the loud siren went off for the winner.

"Damn, Cherish, I see you hitting a little over there on the slots. Maybe I should get up from this coin drinker and move next to you so some of that luck can rub off on me." Divine smiled as he got up to be nosey and see how much Cherish had hit for.

"Hell naw! Stay your losing ass over there. Someone has to lose, and I don't want your bad luck ass over here by me messing up the few dollars I'm winning 'cause I need them."

"Girl, shut up," Divine replied, as the attendant brought Cherish $2,000 in cash and turned her light off. "Maybe I can hit over here," he said, moving a few seats down from Cherish to try another slot machine.

Damn, she's attractive, Divine thought, as a light-skinned lady

Deaubrey Devine

took a seat next to him with her friend.

"Excuse me, handsome. Are you having any luck on these machines?" asked Faith.

"Hell naw! Shit, I'm just here giving out donations on these damn machines. I'm sure you'll do much better than the loser over here," replied Divine.

"Yeah, right. Well, how's your wife doing over there?" asked Faith, attempting to find out who the woman was with Divine.

"Wife? Shit, I wish I was married," laughed Divine.

"Dang, don't kill me. My bad, your girlfriend then." Faith smiled and giggled, while trying to pump Divine for information about his female friend.

"Sweetie, that's my cousin, Cherish," said Divine. "Cuz, she thought we were married," yelled Divine to Cherish. "My name is Divine." He smiled as he stuck out his hand to shake the woman's hand, while asking her name.

"My name is Faith, and this is my home girl Misty," she replied.

"Nice to meet y'all. What brings y'all to the Bahamas?" asked Divine, trying to find out about the women.

"Well, we just got our bonus money from closing a big sales deal, and we wanted to get away for a few days to celebrate. And what brings you and your little girlfriend slash play cousin on the low to the Bahamas?" smiled Faith.

"You just gonna make me be all booed up, huh?" chuckled Divine, giving a smirk to the beautiful, hazel-eyed, slender woman. "I'm here with my cousin Cherish because she received a free trip from her parents," replied Divine.

"Oh, I get it. The secret business trip out of town so no one can tell you two are together. Your secret is safe with me. I'll throw away the key," smiled Faith, as she looked at Divine, who shook his head.

"Alright, Faith, shit. You can cut that conversation short because a bitch is hungry and needs to eat something," interrupted Misty, who was jealous because she wasn't getting any attention.

"Okay, I'm coming," replied Faith. "So, Divine, what are y'all doing later?"

"I may roll solo to the club nearby because cuz is into the church thing and doesn't go out," responded Divine.

"Well, we wanted to go out, too. So, we'll meet you there to give you some company if you don't mind a few tagalongs," said Faith, as she picked up her purse and gave Divine twenty dollars. "Here, Boo, make sure you hit big because I want a two-karat tennis bracelet and a few drinks tonight," she said before walking off to catch up with Misty, who had already walked out the casino.

"Cherish, did you see the girl give me twenty dollars?" asked Divine, turning to Cherish in shock.

"Yeah, I saw that trick. That scam may be up to something and want something in return in the long run," replied Cherish with a disgusted look.

"Man, lil momma was kinda cute, with her little petite ass. I may have to see what she's about later," replied Divine.

"Boy, you better leave that damn girl alone because she's up to no good, being bold like that to just come up to you," warned Cherish. "Are you ready to go? I'm kind of tired, and I want to go back to the room to read a little."

"Yeah, we can leave. I want to go back and get ready for the club anyway," responded Divine, as the two rose to leave.

After dressing, Divine left out for the club, where he met up with Faith who was by herself.

"Where's your home girl?" asked Divine.

"Oh, Misty's in the bed sleep. She's upset with her boyfriend back home in Houston, so she wasn't up for going out tonight," replied Faith, as she thought, *Damn, I hope that bitch doesn't wake up from those sleeping pills I crushed up and put in her drink when she was eating.* "So let's forget about Cherish and Misty and have some fun. Come on. Let's go to the bar and get some drinks," suggested Faith, leading the way.

"I didn't win enough for the tennis bracelet, but I got you covered for a few drinks," smiled Divine, as they approached the bar.

"Silly, don't worry. I'll pay for the first few rounds," replied Faith.

Over the next couple of hours, the two went back and forth from the dance floor to the bar, where they took turns paying for their drinks. As the two grew tipsy, they both started feeling each song the D.J. played. On one particular song, Divine began to grip her soft ass with both of his hands to pull her as close to him as he could.

"Damn, baby, your ass is so soft," whispered Divine in Faith's ear, as he cuffed her left shoulder blade with his right arm and slid his left hand under her short silk mini skirt to feel her bare ass, which was free of panties.

"Damn, you're making my pussy so wet," replied the horny, hot, and aggressive Faith, as she turned around on the crowded dance floor, took his left hand, and placed it on her aqua warm pussy.

What the fuck, thought Divine, as he began fingering Faith right on the dance floor, while a crowd of guys looked on closely.

When Faith noticed the guys staring, she decided to give them a good show by pushing her ass back on Divine's bulging manhood and grinding hard from side to side, while losing herself in the music. As Divine was fingering her and looking at the guys while smiling, Faith grabbed Divine's left hand out her creamy pussy and started sucking her juices off his thick, fat fingers like she was sucking on a lollipop.

"Fuck naw! Did you see that shit, son? That's an easy fuck, yo," said one of the guys, as they hit each other and went crazy while witnessing the event.

Damn, this bitch is freaky, thought Divine, as he slid his finger in and out of Faith's mouth.

Faith then opened her eyes to look at the guys, before taking Divine's fingers to insert them back inside her pussy, while looking at the guys and mouthing the words, "So tasty," real slow with her eyes squinted as she licked her lips. She then turned around to face Divine and stuck her pierced tongue in his mouth. The two wrapped each other in their arms tight and tongued in front of everyone, not caring who looked because they didn't know any of the people around.

"Finger this good pussy, baby. I want you to wear it out in the bathroom or after the club tonight."

"Yeah, lil momma, you want me to put something on your ass tonight, huh?" replied Divine, with a confident smile, as he began to suck on the right side of Faith's neck while pulling her close by her hair.

"Come on. Let's go get a drink," said Faith unexpectedly, as she grabbed his hand and walked to the bar.

Faith ordered a drink with extra ice and then asked Divine did he want something.

"I'm good," he replied.

"What's wrong?" asked Faith.

"Man, I'm good. I'm just blown because you're freaky as hell, and I love that in a woman," responded Divine, as he smiled.

"This is me, boo. I aim to please. Are you shy?" asked Faith.

"Naw, why did you ask me that?"

"No reason," responded Faith, while looking around the club to scope out the scene as she waited on the bartender to bring her drink. Suddenly, she straddled Divine and began unzipping his pants.

"What are you doing?" asked Divine.

"Look," said Faith, as she pushed firmly down on Divine's thighs and gave him direct eye contact, "I asked you if you were shy."

"And I told you no, I'm not," responded Divine, as he thought to himself, *What the fuck is wrong with this crazy bitch?*

Speechless, he could only look on as Faith pulled his dick out, covered it with his long shirt, and began to stroke his dick up and down while looking him in the eyes.

"Are you stingy with the dick?" asked Faith.

"Hell naw. What's up?"

"Well, play with my pussy. No one's looking over here at us in this dark area," said Faith, as Divine took his right hand and started to play with Faith's wet pussy. "Divine, stick your fingers in my mouth. Let me taste those fruit juices."

What the hell, thought Divine, placing his fingers in Faith's mouth.

Once she had sucked them clean, she took her drink to the head and drank it down, while continuing to stroke him. Then, she took one of the ice cubes from the glass in her mouth and said, "I wanna please you so much."

Pulling his shirt back, she bent over and started sucking his dick right there at the bar.

After looking around to see who was looking, Divine looked down at Faith, while trying to pull the drunken lady up from his lap. "Relax, baby," she said, while looking him directly in the eyes. "Fuck these people." Faith picked up where she left off, giving Divine slow head as his eyes opened and closed.

"Come on, Faith. Stop. Let's go back to the hotel," he finally said, pulling her up again just as the bartender walked over, catching the tail end of the oral performance.

"Damn, don't stop the freak show," shouted the bartender, as Divine took the staggering Faith by the hand and led her out the club so they could hail a cab.

During the drive back to the hotel, Faith leaned over and placed her mouth over Divine's hard dick, which she had again released from the confines of his pants.

Faith stopped her oral pleasing long enough to say, "Driver, if you can speed this ride up, there's a big tip coming your way."

CHAPTER 2

As the cab pulled up to the hotel where the both of them were staying, Divine paid the driver and told the staggering Faith that he would walk her to her room and then leave. He didn't want to show disrespect by taking advantage of her while she was drunk. However, when they reached her room, she began to fake like she was sick and about to pass out, and asked Divine to stay for a few minutes.

"So when are you leaving?" she asked, sitting on the side of the bed.

"We're leaving tomorrow morning," replied Divine, taking a seat next to her.

"I wish we were. I'm getting bored here. We're supposed to leave on Tuesday," Faith said, as Divine looked at her.

To be honest, he really didn't care when she was leaving because he didn't want to get to know her.

"What type of work do you do? What types of things do you like to do?" asked Faith, getting personal with her line of questioning.

I wish she would shut the hell up. I don't even know her. I'm just concerned about her because I'm partly responsible for the condition she's in, thought Divine. "Look, Faith, just chill and relax. If you start feeling sick when I leave, you may have to wake up your girlfriend," he said, trying to cut the conversation short.

Damn, it's now or never, thought Faith, as she began to take off her clothes and do an exotic dance for Divine all around the room.

"You better stop acting so damn wild before you wake up Misty."

"Believe me, Misty's out for the count. She sleeps really hard," replied Faith, before walking over, pushing him back on the bed, pulling off his pants, and starting to suck his dick.

As Divine laid back, Faith reached in the nightstand drawer and

15

pulled out a condom and a dildo the size of a jack hammer.

"What the fuck are you going to do with that big shit?" shouted Divine with a surprised look on his face.

"Oh, baby, don't be alarmed. This is my boyfriend that wants to join in. His name is Big Daddy, and he's no joke with the hemi engine in him," replied Faith.

"Faith, you're a wild girl," responded Divine, as he watched Faith play with herself with Big Daddy.

Faith then pushed Divine back on the bed, lubed his penis with her saliva, and started sliding her tongue ring up and down the shaft, slurping loudly while doing so. With Divine's hands on the back of her neck, she tore open a condom package and put the condom in her mouth.

"What do you want to do with this hard, long dick?" asked Divine as he looked closely at Faith.

"Shhh," responded Faith, as she went back down for more.

Divine's dick wiggled and tingled as he watched Faith perform a trick he had never witnessed before.

"Gotdamn, girl, that's some circus shit," Divine said, when he noticed the condom that was once in her mouth was now on his dick.

"Are you going to stay with me tonight or go back to the room with your cousin?" asked Faith seductively, while giving him intense eye contact and proceeding to suck the head of his dick. The veins in his penis looked like they were about to explode.

"It all depends on how many times you can make this dick cum," responded Divine, suddenly forgetting his disinterest in knowing her. "Come here," he said, as he aggressively turned Faith around so she could ride his dick backwards. Upon doing so, he noticed Misty's name tattooed on her lower back.

"What the fuck is Misty's name doing tattooed on you?" asked Divine in a tone of curiosity and disbelief.

"Boy, that's a damn fake tattoo," replied Faith quickly, lying off the top of her head as she lowered her wet pussy down on his dick and began riding it slowly. "We got each other's names tatted on us so we could pretend to be lesbians in an attempt to ward off any guys who we were not interested in being approached by," she explained, while continuing her slow, up and down pace. "Oooh, baby, fuck the tattoo. Talk to me as I ride your big, thick dick. Damn, it feels so good in my pussy," said Faith, as she began to loosen up, enjoying

Divine's tool as it penetrated inside of her.

"That's it. Work it just like that," Divine said, while placing both of his thumbs near the outside of her pussy lips and palming her soft ass cheeks like they were a pair of sponges, which caused her ass to spread and her pussy to open while his dick gently slid in and out. "That's it, Faith. Ride this dick. Make that pussy nut."

He aggressively pulled Faith's butt checks down towards him, as he squeezed his butt muscles together to throw his hips upwards as he penetrated in and out of her. Then, he began smacking her right butt cheek with a firm slap of his hand.

"Now you better ride this hard dick to the Goddess" commanded Divine as Faith winded and worked her hips on his dick.

"I will, daddy. Just keep it going deeper," replied Faith, while working her hips on his dick.

"Gotdamn, baby, I want this wet pussy to feel all this dick," said Divine, as he repositioned himself on his heels so he could penetrate her deeper from behind.

"Ooww! I do, Divine!" screamed Faith with a weak cry, as she took her knees off the bed so she could get on her tippy toes and throw her pussy back at him at a faster pace.

"Let me feel that tight kitty from the back," Divine panted.

"Come on, baby. Have it your way. Beat this pussy up. You can have it," replied Faith.

Divine started penetrating her deeper, faster, and harder as the liquor began to kick in, giving him a hard, bold cock that wouldn't bend.

As he began pulling and pushing Faith back and forth away from him, while hitting it from the back, Faith said, "That's it. Fuck me, baby. Fuck me with that dick going all the way up in me."

Not able to hold back any longer, she released her juices all over Divine's pubic hairs.

"Come on, baby. Stick that ass up," said Divine, as he slapped her ass cheeks hard, before placing his hands on her shoulders and pulling her into him so she could take every inch of his dick.

"Yes, cum, Divine," Faith screamed, while gripping the sheets, and as if on cue, he erupted like a volcano.

After pulling out, Divine quickly went into the bathroom to avoid facing the awkward situation he had allowed himself to be sucked into.

Damn, this girl is a freak, Divine thought, as he removed the condom, wrapped it in some tissue, and flushed it down the toilet.

Upon emerging from the bathroom, Faith was waiting right outside the door.

"Damn, that was some good-ass sex," said Faith. "So how do you feel about me since we made love after only a few hours of knowing each other?"

What do you think? And besides, that wasn't making love; that was a fuck, Divine thought, while trying to think of a way to escape the confines of her room without her tripping.

"Do you think we have a future?" continued Faith, as Divine continued to ignore her.

He wanted nothing more than to move around her, make his way out the door, and get as far away from her emotional ass as possible.

Unfazed by his lack of response, Faith proceeded to bombard her new prized possession with questions. "Are you dating anyone? When do you think we'll see each other again? When do you want to meet my family?"

What the fuck? I don't even know your last name, he thought. But, instead, he responded, "Soon…whenever…just let me know, baby.

Just then, Misty started to stir underneath her covers.

"Divine, you better go ahead and leave before Misty wakes up and thinks I'm a slut for sleeping with you on the first night. And please don't say anything to anyone about what we did," said a frigid Faith as she tried to rush Divine out the room.

"You don't have to worry about that. Remember, what goes on in the Bahamas stays in the Bahamas," smiled Divine as he gathered his clothes so he could dress before going back to his room to meet his cousin Cherish.

He quickly exited with no thoughts of leaving his number for her. He just wanted to get away from Faith and forget he had ever seen her.

The next day, Divine ventured out of his room to explore the cruise ship, while Cherish decided to try her luck on the gambling tables. After walking around the boat for a few hours, he returned to the lobby where he fell asleep to the rocking waves of the ocean.

In what seemed like only a few seconds later, Divine was

awakened by a voice saying, "Round two," and as he opened his eyes, he found Faith staring down at him. He prayed it was a nightmare, but to his dismay, he was very much awake.

"What's up, Faith?" said Divine in a shallow voice, his face frowned up.

"Wow! I thought I would have never seen you again because we didn't exchange numbers. This is just ironic for us to meet up again on this big ship," replied Faith with a wicked smirk on her face. "Well, let me get your number so we can stay in touch with each other," she said, while reaching in her purse to retrieve her cell phone. *Man, I don't wanna keep in touch with your ass. It was only a one-night stand. Get over it,* thought Divine, as he called off a fake number, which she repeated back to make sure she had saved it in her phone correctly.

"So what are you about to do now?" asked Faith, while placing her phone back in her purse.

"I'm going to the upper deck to lie out for a few minutes, watch the sunset, and feel the motion from the ocean," Divine replied, hoping his response would not be something Faith wanted to do, too.

"Cool, I was going to watch the ocean view from the railing on the second floor, but your idea sounds much better. Come on," said Faith, as she led the way to the upper deck.

"Scoot over a little," she said after Divine stretched out on one of the deck chairs.

As if they had known each other for some time, she positioned herself next to him, placed his left arm around her shoulder, and cuddled up close beside him.

Damn, this girl is tripping, thought Divine as he laid there. *This boat needs to turn on the jets, and hurry up and get back to shore.*

"So where's your cousin?" she asked.

"She wanted to go hit up the casino, but I wasn't in the mood to give my money away," he replied.

"I'm not much of a gambler myself, but I do like to play the lottery from time to time. So why don't you bring me some luck and give me a good 4-digit number I can play when I get back home?"

Not thinking much of his response, Divine quickly blurted out "0220", which was a very significant number for him. Faith stored that number in her memory bank for reasons unknown to her at the time, and then quickly changed the subject to a more personal matter.

"Do you have children, or would you ever want children?" asked Faith.

"No children yet, but I plan to have some whenever I make that special woman my wife," replied Divine.

"I'm in need of a good man after being hurt in my past relationships with lame men," Faith said, before lifting her head up toward the sky, which now had a slightly dark hue as nighttime approached. "Divine, look at that star shining down on us."

"I see it," responded Divine, not paying attention to the star, but only responding in hopes that she would be quiet.

"Divine, I wish upon that one star that we will never separate ever," she continued, while pushing her butt on Divine, hoping to get a quickie before the boat docked. "Do you wish the same?"

"Yeah," replied Divine, although his wish was to get as far away from her psychotic ass as possible.

Just then, the ship's captain came on the P.A. system to announce that the ship was approaching their destination in Miami. His prayers had been answered.

"Alright, Faith, it was nice meeting and hanging out with you. Make sure you hit me up, sexy," Divine said, while standing up so he could find Cherish and depart from the boat, making distance between him and Faith.

"Here's my phone number," she said, stopping him in his tracks and handing him one of her business cards.

Before he could get too far, she pulled out her phone to call his cell phone and discovered she had been duped. After putting her phone on silent so its ring would not be audible, she called out to Divine.

"Hey, Divine, may I use your phone for a second to call my ride? I forgot to charge my freakin' phone and it's dead."

"Sure," Divine replied, while walking back to her and handing over his phone, oblivious to her tricks.

"Thank you, sweetie," Faith said, as she returned the phone to him after acting like she had placed a call for someone to pick her up.

"Alright, see ya," Divine responded, while walking away quickly and breathing a sigh of relief since he knew once he returned to Atlanta he would never have to lay eyes on Faith again.

CHAPTER 3

"Divine, can you stop at a rest area so I can use the restroom?" asked Cherish.

"Okay, I gotcha," replied Divine, as he pulled over at a gas station a few miles up the interstate to get gas and stretch. *I might as well check my voicemail messages while I'm waiting,* Divine thought, noticing he had new voice messages.

"First new message," the automated voice announced.

My birthday weekend is coming up and I want to hang out and receive my big gift from you.

"Next new message."

I miss you and need some...bad.

"Next new message."

I've been extremely busy, but I miss tripping with you and hearing your crazy stories. Call me.

"Next new message."

I'll be in town about eight o'clock tonight and want you to come visit, if you're available, which I'm hoping you are.

While deleting the messages, Divine thought, *Damn, I got all these women trying to pull me from different angles. Sometimes I wish I wasn't such a player. Sexing all these girls and using them with no strings attached...hell, this shit is getting costly and becoming stressful.*

Before he could place his phone back in its holster, it rang.

"Whaddup, D? How was the trip, and where's my bighead sister?" asked Danny Boy, not giving Divine a chance to answer. "Man, it's on in a few weeks for my Let It Snow all-white party at Club Seven."

"Bitch, you crazy. Remember what happened the last time you

threw that birthday bash a few years ago. Your damn wife came to the party and saw you dancing all on them hoes. Your stupid ass almost got a divorce behind that stupid shit. I must admit, though, the party was the shit," responded Divine.

"I know right! That shit was thick as hell, but this time, I've got it covered. I'm sending my wife on vacation to Las Vegas and covering all the costs for the weekend, including an extra three grand in her pocket to shop with. D, you should see her ass around her. She's so damn happy. She's up here packing shit already," laughed Danny Boy, as he told his cousin his plan.

"Well, bitch, I don't agree with it and can't tell you what to do with your marriage, but hell, let's party like we've never partied before, big dawg, if you got your shit together," replied Divine.

"I've already been spreading the word around town, but you need to help me put flyers up and pass them out at the barbershops, salons, and all the rest of the hot spots. We need to have this party banging as one of the hottest parties of the year," said Danny Boy.

"I got ya. Just leave whatever you need me to pass out up front at the apartment desk or you can drop them off this week," Divine replied.

"Alright. Oh shit, I almost forgot, Divine. Hey, boy, you just may have you a nice piece of ass you use to love to eat show up at the party, so get your tongue in training to act a fool in the pussy," said Danny Boy, as he cracked up laughing.

"Nigga, who? Shit, what's up? You got me thinkin' hard over here," responded Divine.

"You'll see at the party. She told me not to say anything because she may not come."

"Man, stop making up shit and get your ass off my phone," Divine said, before hanging up on Danny Boy.

Dang, I missed a call. I've never seen this number before.

Cherish got back in the vehicle, as he started driving back home.

Damn, I hope I didn't miss out on the shorty I met at the Underground. She's going to be my new cutie pie, Divine thought, while listening to the phone ring after calling the number back.

"Hello," a sweet, sexy voice answered.

"Hello. How are you? Did someone just call Divine's number a few seconds ago?" he asked, hoping the female would state her name because he had forgotten it.

"Hold on," responded the beautiful voice.

"Hello," said another familiar voice Divine had heard before.

"Hello. Did someone call Divine from this number?"

"Naw, baby, no one called you, but you called my cousin back from when I used your phone to check on my ride," replied Faith.

"Damn," said Divine, hitting the steering wheel. He was pissed off to say the least. "Oh, I'm sorry. I was just trying to return the call. I don't mean to be a bother."

"You're cool, Divine. I'll make sure I hit you up when I get back home to Houston," she replied.

"Alright," said Divine, as he hung up the phone. "Cuz, damn, I done called Faith back on accident. Now she has my real number," he told Cherish, as he hit her on the leg to tell her about the incident.

"Just tell her not to call you anymore. This is how men start leading women on to believe things and get them all wrapped up in them, when they could have been upfront from the jump," replied Cherish.

"Dang, she's cool people, but I just didn't want another out-of-town friend I can't keep in touch with and see when I want," responded Divine, as he continued talking with Cherish for a few hours before she fell asleep.

"Neal, what's up? What are you doing, brother?" asked Divine to his good friend and co-worker who lived next door to him.

"I'm just chilling," replied Neal.

"Let me put my bags inside, and I'll be over in a few minutes with a blunt to hangout for a prayer meeting before I go to work on the overnight shift. I have to get my mind right for the security guard job for the gated complex out here."

After going over to Neal's apartment, Divine told him about Faith, as they smoked a few blunts and laughed. Not long after, there was a knock at the door, and Neal got up to open the door and let Lemon Head in, who was a friend of the fellas and a functioning alcoholic who held a job as a flight attendant.

"Man, I'm leaving so ya'll can chill," laughed Divine, as he got up to head home.

"Yeah, bitch. Haul ass and lock the door behind you," said Neal, as watched Divine leave to head back to his apartment.

After an hour of watching a basketball game on television,

Divine's doorbell rang. He thought it was his friend from the voicemail that said she missed him and needed some.

Damn, I told her to come over for a quickie before I went in to work, but I didn't know she would be this early, Divine said to himself as he opened the door. "Man, Lemon Head, what do you want?" asked Divine upon seeing her standing on the other side.

"Look, bitch, I just came over to get a shot of gin from your bar," replied Lemon Head.

"Girl, go ahead and get you three shots," said Divine.

"Damn, D, you must want me to get loose," she responded.

"Hell naw! You gotta get that ass in gear to get the fuck out. I got company coming over in a few," said Divine, as he thought, *I do want some of that good head, though.*

"I'll be back through to suck you dry," responded Lemon Head out the blue with confidence.

"Alright," smiled Divine, as he watched Lemon Head grab her plastic cup of straight gin and walk outside.

"Let me go shower for work and get ready," said Divine as he turned around to head for the shower, but he didn't get far before the doorbell rang again. "Let me open the door for my baby!" shouted Divine loudly so the person who he thought it was could hear the comment. "Man, what in the hell do you want now, girl?"

"Calm down. I left my keys by the bar, and I have to use the restroom real quick," Lemon Head replied.

Next, the phone rang. It was his expected company calling to say she wouldn't be able make it and would have to come another time.

"Okay, it's getting late anyway," responded Divine.

After hanging up, he went to see why Lemon Head was taking so long in the bathroom. As he approached the doorway, he saw Lemon Head laughing and attempting to brush her teeth with a rag, with the toothpaste and water running down her arm.

"Girl, get your high ass out of the bathroom," he told her, as they started to laugh. "What's up?" Divine asked, while pulling out his dick. He seized the opportunity to relieve some of his horniness, especially since his company couldn't make it.

"Dang, Divine, you're sweaty. Go wipe off, and I'll be in the living room waiting."

After taking a quick shower, Divine returned to the living room to see Lemon Head flipping through the channels on the television. No words needed to be spoken. Immediately, Lemon Head went to work, grabbing his dick and sucking it, while the blood rushed from Divine's feet and head to cause the ultimate erection.

Lemon Head moaned as she sucked a few times on his penis, before stopping and pulling Divine's dick out of her mouth.

"D, I sleep with you, Neal, and Danny Boy because I can't find a good man," explained Lemon Head, interrupting his ecstasy. "But, you sleep with all of these women, so why don't you settle down and have a main girl?"

"I don't have a girl because no one wants me," replied Divine as he guided his dick back in her mouth so she could continue with her oral performance.

However, after a few more sucks, Lemon Head felt the need to explain further for her actions.

"I do what you want me to do with your boys because I care about you," said Lemon Head.

Man, suck this dick, trick, and shut up with all that shit, he thought, as he listened.

"And, yeah right, about no one wanting you. I know everyone wants Divine, including the one who he looks down on while she sucks his dick in a sour way," she added, before finishing off what she started.

Over the next few days, Faith tried to call and text Divine, but he didn't respond to her calls or text back. One night, while at work, Divine got a little tired, so he asked Neal to keep watch while he reclined in his chair to take a quick nap. As Neal talked on the phone with his girlfriend, Divine slept through the slow traffic that passed through the gated community. However, he wasn't sleep for long, before his phone rang, waking him out of his sleep.

"Hello," answered Divine, not looking at the caller ID.

"Well, hello, Divine," replied Faith.

Damn, Divine said to himself, as he held the phone away from his ear for a moment. "Why are you calling me so late?" he finally asked.

"I figured I could catch you at this time of night since you don't answer my calls during the day," replied Faith. "Please don't be upset with me."

"You're cool. Don't worry about it. I was just here at work anyway," Divine responded.

"I had a delay on a sale at work, but I'm just glad I made it through the crazy day. I sure could have used a friend's voice of reason today," she said.

"I know how that real estate business can be sometimes, with you depending on those checks. You can hit me up anytime, and I'll get back to you when I get a chance."

"Well, I just called to tell you that and to hear your voice before I went to sleep. Make time for me soon, or else I'm going to kick your ass if you don't," Faith laughed.

"I will, and I miss you," he replied, just to make Faith feel special.

"I miss you more. If I make it with my sales, I'm going to treat you to a candlelight dinner with dancing. So, dust off your dancing shoes, baby boy," Faith added.

"I'll be praying for you," replied Divine.

"Thank you. I'll hit you later this week," Faith responded, as she hung up the phone.

Maybe she's not so deranged after all, Divine thought, as he relieved Neal so he could take his nap, as the two often alternated doing on their overnight shift together.

CHAPTER 4

As the days passed and the week of Danny Boy's "Let It Snow" all-white party came, Faith flew into Atlanta that Wednesday to go job hunting. She wanted to search for a job in the Chocolate City where the real estate industry was hot and also pay Divine a surprise visit. After Faith picked up her rental car and checked into the Westin Hotel, she called Divine to say hello. When he didn't answer, Faith texted him to see if he would like to go out on a date near the Lenox Mall in Buckhead.

After waking up that evening from his nap, Divine saw he had missed Faith's call, and decided to return it to see what was up.

"Hey, I was sleep when you called. How are you?" Divine asked when she answered.

"I'm doing fine. How are you?" replied Faith.

"I'm still a little tired and hungry. I'm on my way to get something to eat from Chops Steakhouse. They have the bomb almond-crusted swordfish, and I try to treat myself there once a month. I've been waiting all day to eat because they're closed for lunch. Hey, maybe you can go with me one day when you come to visit."

"When I come to visit, huh? So can you treat me to dinner today?" asked Faith.

"Sure, I'm on Paces Ferry," Divine replied sarcastically, thinking Faith was still somewhere in Houston and joking around about joining him.

"Well, thank you. I'll just meet you there after I call 411 to get directions to the restaurant from where I am," said Faith.

"Okay, boo. I'll be waiting," Divine laughed, as he hung up and proceeded to go inside the restaurant to order take-out for the evening.

As Divine stood in line to order his food, Faith walked in the door and squeezed Divine's right butt cheek.

"May I order some vitamin D?" she asked in a sexy voice.

"What the fuck!" shouted Divine out of shock, as he turned around to see Faith looking gorgeous in her black evening silk dress and high heels. "Damn, how did you get down here so fast? Last time we spoke, you said you weren't coming for a few months."

"Well, I wanted to surprise you," replied Faith.

Shit, I can't believe this bitch done popped up way from Houston without a warning, Divine thought, as he told the cashier to give him a menu so Faith could place her order.

After Faith ordered, Divine told the cashier to have the waiter send the food to a table so they could sit down and dine. Divine walked with Faith to the table, where they sat down and ordered a few drinks to kick back and converse over dinner. After dinner, Divine asked Faith where she was staying, hoping she didn't assume she could stay at his place. That just couldn't happen. He could risk her messing up his player's circle and rotation of the days that he saw his different women.

"I'm staying at the Westin Hotel and Resorts. I've stayed there before," replied Faith.

"Oh, okay. Well, can a brother come there to swim or something? I heard they have some great amenities. I may need to come hangout at the hotel," Divine said, not giving Faith enough time to ask if they could go back to his apartment so she could find out where he lived.

After Faith followed behind Divine in her car back to the hotel, Divine parked and then entered Faith's car, sitting in the passenger's seat. As they hugged, he slid his hand under her dress to feel her butt as he kissed her, but Faith stopped him abruptly.

"I'm on my period," she said, while pushing Divine's hand away.

Damn, I wish you would have told me this shit earlier before I came over here, thought Divine. "That's cool," Divine replied, trying to play off the rejection. "We don't need to be doing this anyway."

"Oh, yes, we do need to be doing it, but now isn't a good time. Besides, I'm not in the room alone. My mom is sharing it with me."

"Your mom?"

"Yeah, my mom came down with me on this trip," responded Faith, as she thought to herself, *Nigga, you believe anything. I'm not on my period and my mom isn't here. I just want to find out where your ass stays, so I can come over to your damn house to see what's really going on when I'm not here.*

"I can't wait until she meets your sexy ass," Faith said, knowing this would run Divine off.

Man, I'm not with this meet-the-parents shit, thought Divine, becoming nervous. "You know what? I need to go on home anyway to shower and get ready for work," said Divine quickly, using the excuse of having to get to work as his reason for not being able to meet her mother at that time.

"Okay, boo. I'm kind of tired myself. All the shopping from earlier with my mother has me drained, so I guess I should turn it in for tonight."

"I enjoyed your company, Faith," Divine said, trying to sound sincere.

"Likewise, Divine," Faith responded, as Divine exited her car and got back in his.

When Divine pulled out of the hotel parking lot, Faith followed a safe distance behind him to his apartment complex where the gate was open. With her headlights out so she wouldn't be detected, she watched as Divine parked and entered an apartment. She then crept slowly to find out the address and apartment number of where she thought Divine lived, before returning to her car and back to the hotel.

A day later, Faith went to a local cookie shop to order Divine some creative cookies and have them sent to his apartment. The following day, while Divine was chilling over at Neal's apartment having a prayer session, the doorbell rang. It was the delivery man with a package to Neal's apartment with Divine's name on it.

Neal he signed for the package, and then turned to Divine and said, "Damn, brah, now you're getting packages delivered to my home. What's next?"

"Man, that's your shit. Quit playing around," responded Divine, as he laughed.

"Naw, D, seriously! The label is address to you. Look right here," Neal said, while extending the package to Divine for him to take it. "Now hurry up and open it."

"Man, let me hold it, with your blind, non-reading, high ass," Divine said, snatching the package from him.

"Yeah, see. I'm not lying, punk, and I know who sent that,"

laughed Neal, teasing his friend.

"Shut up!" replied Divine, as he opened up the box to see the expressive message on the designed cookie.

Divine felt somewhat cared about because he never had a woman send him a love token through the mail, especially without a specific occasion.

"Alright, now that you've read the damn cookie can I get a piece?" asked Neal. "I got the fuckin' munchies, nigga."

"Here, greedy." Divine handed him the cookie before reading the note enclosed.

Hi, baby. I enjoyed the time we shared together and hope this is the beginning of something awesome. As you read this card, just open up your arms to catch the love I'm sending to you. I'm completely off code red, so hopefully, this evening we can get together and I can show you a trick I can do when I dress up as a construction worker. I really want you to put the soft thing in the cement mixer to make that thing so hard and stiff.

"I have to find a way to hang out with Faith, but without her being so nosey and persistent. She has already violated my damn privacy by popping up," vented Divine after reading the note.

"Man, I don't know what you're going to do, but you need to get rid of her ass before that party tomorrow. You know Danny Boy has those bad-ass promotional parties with the fire-ass D.J. that spins that good music and keeps the crowd on the dance floor all night. Damn, I can't wait. You know them hoes gonna be in there dressed all up, looking good," Neal explained excitedly.

"I know. I just have to find a way to tell Faith something so her ass won't be trying to follow me or pop up at the damn party. She doesn't even know I'm going to the party tomorrow."

Just then, the doorbell rang again, and Neal opened the door without asking who it was, a bad habit of his.

"Hey, may I help you?" asked Neal to the woman who stood there.

"Damn," Divine said, as he peeped around Neal's body.

"I'm here to see my sweetie," replied Faith, while Divine tried to hide the ashtray with the roaches in them. He didn't want Faith to think he was a pothead.

"I can't believe ya'll were hittin' the J and didn't pass it to a sister," Faith said, as she walked in, noticing Divine trying to hide the evidence of what they had been doing.

"Now you're my kind of girl, slim. What's your name? I'm Neal."

"My name is Faith, and it's nice to meet you," replied Faith.

"Oooh, okay. I can now put a face with a name. I've heard so much about you. Divine always talks about you."

I wish blabbermouth would shut the fuck up and stop putting extra stuff in this girl's head, thought Divine as he listened to Neal trying to be funny.

"Oh yeah, baby? Well, I missed you," smiled Faith, as she walked over to Divine and gave him a hug and a kiss on the cheek.

Divine felt obligated to respond in a positive way after receiving his little surprise in the mail.

"I missed you, too," Divine replied in a very shallow voice. "But, Faith, you can't just be popping up over here like this to visit me. I'm actually getting ready to leave in a little while."

"I'm sorry to pop up, but I've been calling your phone and you didn't answer. I was just in the area doing a little shopping and wanted to drop off this shirt I got for you while I was on this side of town," responded Faith.

"My bad. My phone is on the charger," Divine replied, as he looked at Neal who was raising his eyebrows like *Fool, go on and make a pimp move to free your ass up for tomorrow.* "Thanks for the gift, Faith. Since I'm hanging out tomorrow with my cousin Danny Boy who's from out of town, you're more than welcome to come with me to this recital I'm attending tonight for this kid that my cousin, who you met on the cruise, used to babysit."

"I would love to go with you. It beats spending time with my mom, and we get to hangout a little before I leave," replied Faith, feeling welcomed into Divine's personal life. "So what should I wear?"

"Just wear something casual. Why don't you go back to your room and get dressed, and I'll pick you up in a few. I need to shower and get ready myself. Thanks again for the shirt. I'll call when I'm on my way," Divine replied, as he hurried Faith to the door. "Alright, suga," said Divine, as he kissed a smiling Faith on the cheek before she left out the door.

"Damn, nigga, you hit that on the first night? She's pretty tight, big dawg," Neal said, giving Divine props.

"Yeah, she's okay. She just kills me with crazy shit, like popping up over here and sending cookies to a damn address I never gave her."

"Boy, you know the women will cling to that good tongue they've gotten attached to if you've licked it the right way," laughed Neal.

"Hell, I haven't even done that to her crazy ass yet," chuckled Divine before leaving to take a shower.

After the recital, Divine and Faith headed back to the hotel to be intimate. Afterwards, Faith needed clarity on where Divine stood with her.

"Divine, I have a question for you, but I need you to be totally honest. Promise me that you'll tell the truth," Faith said, while looking over at Divine, who was lying beside her.

Oh shit, here we go with these damn questions again, thought Divine, as he replied, "What's up, boo?"

"Are you in a relationship? I don't know if you are or not, but I got this feeling that you're not telling me something."

"I knew that's what you were going to ask me. No, I'm not in a relationship. I don't want to play kiddy games or be hurt. I just keep myself busy and stay lonely. I wish I could find that right woman, though," he replied.

"I believe you. Just so you know, I feel the exact same way," expressed Faith.

"It's tough and sad, but real. Maybe it will happen soon. It's hard to believe that a woman like you is single," said Divine.

"Yeah, but I don't think either of us will be single much longer. It's not a coincidence that we met miles away and made love the way we did. It's like we just clicked right off the bat."

"That is crazy how that happened," responded Divine, as he thought, *Man, this damn girl always taking shit directly to heart and turning it around to be official towards a relationship.* "Look, I'm gonna get up to head home so I can be on time for my job. I don't want to get fired for being late. I'll give you a call, and maybe we can hang on Sunday. Don't forget, I'll be with my cousin all day tomorrow," Divine reminded her, while getting dressed.

"Okay, boo," Faith replied, as she spotted his hat that had fallen on the side of the bed, but which went unnoticed by Divine. She thought to herself, *Bump that cousin for a few minutes tomorrow. I have to get me some of that hickory sausage a few more times before I leave; and I know just the excuse to use to get it.*

On the day of Danny Boy's all-white party, Divine and Neal woke up to go have breakfast and hit the Lenox Mall to get some nice all-white suits and shoes for the dress-to-impress bash. When they finished getting their elegant attire from the men's fashion store, the two went for a fresh cut at the barbershop, where they saw flyers and listened to everyone talk about the party that night. After hitting the CD spot to get some new music, the liquor store to get right during the pre-party, and getting their cars detailed, they returned home.

"Danny Boy, what's up?" said Divine to his cousin, who showed up to the apartment to give him VIP passes for the party.

"Whaddup, fool? How's it going, Neal?" Danny Boy replied, as the guys began to update each other on their families before tripping out over old times and events, while engaging in their familiar prayer meeting and half-watching a comedy movie.

"Alright, fellas, I'm gonna go home so I can get ready to head over to the club. I'll see you guys in a few," said Danny Boy, as he left a few hours later.

"Yeah, D, I'm leaving, too," Neal said, following the exit of Danny Boy.

"Neal, Precious is stopping by for a minute and has one of her friends with her. Are you down to meet her?" asked Divine.

"Come on, D. You know I don't mind, but how does she look?" asked Neal.

"I don't know. Precious is tough, though, so I'm assuming her friend is a bad girl, also."

"I'm down. When are they coming through?"

"They should be here any minute according to the time that she told me when we spoke," Divine replied, while glancing at the clock on the wall.

"Alright then, I'll sit tight and see what's up with her."

About a half hour later, the doorbell rang.

"Man, Divine, if that girl is fucked up, I'm going to haul ass on you, so don't trip," Neal said, as they both laughed.

"Shhh! Be quiet before your blind date hears us, dumb ass," Divine said, as he opened the door after looking out the peephole.

"What's up, butter cup?" said Divine, greeting Precious.

"Hey, handsome, this is my girl," Precious replied, introducing Divine to her dark-skinned heavyset friend who was holding a newborn baby.

"Hello, Divine, nice to meet you," her friend said.

"Likewise," replied Divine, as he smiled and turned to Neal, who was looking straight ahead at the television like he didn't hear any company enter the apartment. "Neal, this is Precious and her friend."

Damn, Precious is fine. Too bad I can't say the same for her friend, Neal thought, before throwing up his hand to wave and then turn his attention back to the movie he was watching.

As Divine and Precious sat on the couch, with Neal sitting in the love seat, the woman with the kid sat in the recliner chair to look at the movie.

"So what's new? I haven't seen you in a few weeks," Divine said.

"I've just been working. I'm sick of my job," replied Precious.

"Why do you say that? You have the perfect personality for the nursing field," complimented Divine.

"I love the people I care for; it's just the racist registered nurse and supervisor that have been there twenty years that I can't stand. I hate when they micro-manage me all the time as an LPN. I try to listen to my peace, which is my gospel music, in my car while on my way to work, but as soon as I enter those workplace doors, the enemy attacks me."

"It will get better when you finish school. You'll be climbing the different nursing level programs sooner than you think," encouraged Divine as he laid back on the couch to hold Precious tight to his body, while thinking, *Damn, this is a straight woman.*

Meanwhile, Faith had pulled up on the scene, exited her car, and went to knock on Neal's apartment door, where she believed Divine actually lived, to return the hat he had left behind in her hotel room the previous night.

"Do you hear that loud knocking on someone's door?" asked Precious, who looked up to notice Divine looking at her. "And why are you looking at me like that?"

"I hear it; just disregard it. I was just daydreaming for a second about ya," Divine replied.

Bam...bam...bam! The knocking on Neal's door grew louder.

"Daydreaming about what? And goodness, they're going to break down that door. You sure you don't want to poke your head outside to see what's going on?"

"I don't care about who's knocking or why. My focus is on you. Precious, I really like you, and I just wanted to know if I can have a piece of this that's been broken?" asked Divine, while pointing to her heart, with her smiling and snuggling closer. "Damn, girl, just a piece. You can donate a piece if you don't wanna give it to me."

"Divine, you know I wouldn't mind giving you whatever you want. It's just bad timing with me and my husband. You know I would get killed if he knew I was even over here. I just like you so much that I can't stay away from you," Precious replied.

"I know. I hate that we didn't meet years ago," sighed Divine.

Outside, Faith was frustrated with getting no response.

Maybe I should ask Divine's neighbors have they seen him, she thought, as she turned to raise her hand to knock on the door that was actually to Divine's apartment.

"Excuse me! You left your lights on!" yelled Lemon Head from the parking lot, just as Faith was about to hit Divine's door.

"Okay, thank you," Faith responded, as she turned to walk back to her car to cut off her lights. "Excuse me," she said, while approaching Lemon Head. "Have you seen Divine? I'm his cousin from out of town. I've been knocking on his door, but he's not answering, and I'm a little concerned."

"I assume he's home. His car is here. What door have you been knocking on?" asked Lemon Head, as Faith pointed to the apartment door on the left. "Sweetie, you have the wrong door. That's his homeboy's Neal's apartment. Divine's apartment is on the right," explained Lemon Head.

"Oh, okay. Thank you," said Faith.

By now, Precious's friend's baby had become restless, so the two women decided it was time for them to leave.

"I'll see you later, D," Precious said, after planting a soft kiss on Divine's lips.

As Precious left out of the apartment, she passed Faith who gave them a mean look, but Precious simply shrugged it off.

No sooner had Divine closed the door, there was knocking similar to that he had heard on Neal's door a short while ago.

"Faith, what the fuck is you doing here?" asked Divine, his mouth dropping in disappointment after opening the door.

"I came to bring your damn hat you left in the room, but I see your ass was in here all cooped up with some other bitches."

"You're really tripping," replied Divine, as Neal came from behind him.

"I'm going to get dressed for the club, D. Excuse me," Neal said, as he walked passed Faith to go to his apartment.

"Why in the fuck are you tripping anyway? That was Neal's people who were just visiting," said Divine, raising his voice to state his case.

"Divine, I'm not stupid. Do you really want me, or do you want to share me? I'll never stop wanting to be yours only, but I will not get mad if you say you're not ready," vented Faith.

"Look, just stop tripping and putting me on the shelf with everyone else. We're friends, and don't ruin that over foolishness," Divine replied, as Faith calmed down and came closer to hug him.

"What club are you going to tonight?"

Damn, Neal, with your big-ass mouth, thought Divine. "Oh, we're going to The Grown Folks' Lounge across town."

"Am I allowed to come?" asked Faith, smiling.

"Sure, just call me when you get there," responded Divine, as he thought to himself, *I'm going to just tell her I couldn't hear my phone in the club when she trips about not being able to find me.* "Well, Faith, I have to shit, shower, and shave to get ready. I'll see you at the lounge," said Divine, getting rid of Faith as she left to get dressed for the party.

CHAPTER 5

"Boy, there are some tight-ass ladies all around this muthafucka tonight. I know my ass gonna get in hella trouble," laughed Danny Boy.

"Man, don't start that. Just do your dirt, and use me and Neal as your usual scapegoat," Divine said.

"I got ya. Where's Neal at anyway?" asked Danny Boy.

"He should already be here or on his way," replied Divine, as they turned around to see that they had talked Neal up.

"Heeyyy," Neal said, as the security finished patting him down.

"Damn, niggas, y'all muthafuckas done got shitty clean to come up in the spot, huh?" commented Danny Boy, while looking the two up and down and checking out their threads.

"Hell, yeah, you gotta have your shit right when you step in one of these grown folks black carpet parties," Neal replied.

"So what's up with the buffet? I'ma need to get a bite," said Divine.

"Your greedy ass ready to get a plate?" Danny Boy responded.

"Hell yeah, I know you have a five-star meal to impress the women," replied Divine.

"You know I gotta do for all the sexy ladies in the house," bragged Danny Boy, as he walked with the guys to the table where they stood in line to wait on the catering service to serve the food. After their plates were piled high, the three men went and sat down at a table covered with a white fabric tablecloth and a nice centerpiece.

Not soon after taking his seat, Divine's phone vibrated with a call from Faith. Of course, he let the phone go straight to his voicemail. *I have to stick to my plan of the party being moved and being too drunk to call to inform her of the changes,* Divine thought, rehearsing the lie in his head. *Also, I have to tell her that I couldn't hear my phone when she was calling because of the loud music in the club.*

Faith exhaled deeply, while standing all dressed up in front of The Grown Folks Lounge, with hopes to party like she did with Divine the Bahamas.

Where is he? This shit is pissing me the hell off, with him not answering his phone, she said to herself, as she stood in the long line for about twenty-five minutes trying to get in the packed club. She looked around and patted her foot impatiently as she called Divine's phone that continued to go to his voicemail.

"I don't know where you are, but you need to come get me because I don't think I'm in the right spot with all of these Spanish people going in the club," Faith said, leaving a message, and then continuing to wait another forty-five minutes in line.

"Alright, only tickets to get in!" yelled the security guard, who stood at the front of the line.

"Tickets? I don't have no damn ticket," Faith said, as she got out of line to approach the security guard. "Excuse me. Can you tell me what's going on at this club tonight?"

"There's a Latino concert going on here tonight, with a professional artist performing," he replied.

"Are there any decent black clubs around here for me to party at tonight?" Faith asked, feeling she was in the wrong place.

"Actually, there's a big all-white party going on at Club Seven. It's been the big hype of the town and airing all over. A former ballplayer named Danny Boy is throwing it across town. He usually goes all out for the mature adults at his parties," replied the security guard, hoping to lead Faith to a good party.

"Okay, thank you," responded Faith, as she walked off. *I see how this bitch wanna try to play me...like I'm some whore that he can buy a few drink for and sleep with on the first night. It's time for me to show him that he needs to be upfront and honest with females, and stop sending mixed signals.*

Meanwhile at Club Seven, Danny Boy's birthday bash was off the chain. The fellas walked up to the V.I.P. area on the stage where the club's director had their reserved table, with the Hennessey, Patron, Grey Goose, and other fine liquors with mixers and ice nearby.

"Man, I'm full from eating and now it's time to get my drink on," Neal said, grabbing a cup to fill with ice before pouring in his liquor, while Divine seized the opportunity to spit game to a beautiful shorty who was passing by.

"Boy, you're still smooth," smiled Neal, after the girl gave Divine her number and walked off.

"I am sometimes. I know a lil sumth'n sumth'n," boasted Divine.

As the night went on, the DJ sent shout outs to the beautiful ladies and handsome gentlemen in the club, and stopped the music a few times so Danny Boy could thank the crowd for coming out to his *Let It Snow* birthday bash. Danny Boy also showed his gratitude by giving away door prizes and goodie bags. The party continued with the drinks flowing and the music spinning.

While Divine and Neal stood next to each other, tipsy from their unlimited drinks, Divine continued to send Faith's calls to his voicemail.

"Divine, let's walk around the club so we can scope out the scene and holler at some more females," Neal suggested.

"Damn, nigga, hold up from all this damn walking in circles like we're at the Daytona 500. Let me check my phone first so I can see who's been hitting me up," Divine said, as he pulled out his phone to see all the missed calls from Faith along with a text message from Precious, who was informing him that she was free from her husband for the night.

While Divine was checking his messages, a very angry and pissed off Faith, who made a trip to Wal-Mart in order to purchase an all-white outfit so she could attend the party, entered the club.

"Where all my old-school grown folks at?" shouted the DJ, playing "Before I Let Go" as the next song.

"Oh shit, boy, do you hear that classic by Frankie Beverly & Maze? That's a good throwback song to get your groove on to," said Divine, while dancing from side to side with an old-school swagger.

"I know, right. Yo, check out that guy in the butterfly-collared white suit dancing with that thick, big booty redbone. Oh my goodness, look at her butt sticking out of her short-ass mini dress," said Neal.

"Wow, you know that guy is going to move on that. He's just too clean up in here, *and* he has a pimp hat on," Danny Boy said, as he watched the two get down on the dance floor.

"I don't know, guys. She may be in here to catch something just like I'm trying to catch something," replied Divine, while making eye contact with the girl. "What's your number?" mouthed Divine as the woman mouthed her digits to him in return.

Neal and Danny Boy simply laughed at him for getting the number while the female was dancing with a guy, but they were not surprised. While Divine was storing her number in his phone, he received a text message.

Damn, you are still sexy as hell. I'm the treat Danny Boy told you about, and I'm sure glad I made it back in town to see your clean, groomed, sexy ass.

Who is this, Divine texted back, not knowing if it was Faith playing games or not.

Do you remember eleven years ago when we got caught by the security guard having sex in the back seat of your car when you came down from college to visit? You better remember me now, responded Hope, Divine's high school sweetheart.

Oh, what's up? Hell yeah, I remember your cute self. Where are you? Come to the V.I.P. section. We're all up here, replied Divine.

Okay, I see you guys. I'm on my way, responded Hope.

"Danny Boy, why didn't you tell me Hope was coming? That was my baby girl," Divine said, flashing a Kool-Aid smile.

"Cuz she told me not to tell you she was coming," replied Danny Boy, as he smiled on the inside, thinking about how the two use to be in love.

"Fellas, I'm gonna go ahead and head home to meet my lil friend," said Neal.

"Alright now, I don't want to come home and see Lemon Head leaving from over there," laughed Divine.

"Man, go 'head with all that before I go get Faith, nigga," threatened Neal jokingly.

"Oh gosh, don't even talk her up. She's been calling me all night."

"Who's Faith?" asked Danny Boy.

"One of my friends. She'll let you beat it on the first night, too, Big Dawg," replied Divine, being funny while bragging on his vacation.

"Where's she at, cuz?" asked Danny Boy, who was ready to step of his marriage box for a new piece.

"Shut up, Divine. You're wild. Oh yeah, and thanks for trying to hook me up with the Atlanta Bears Mascot," Neal said before walking off, referring to Precious' friend.

"I'm grown now. I know a lot more now than I did in my younger days when you popped my little ol' cherry," said Hope, as she came up behind Divine and squeezed his ass.

"Wow! Gotdamn, you're still beautiful," said the star struck Divine, turning around to see the all grown up Hope, who was sparkling like a super model, with pretty white teeth, rich and creamy smooth skin, and not a single scar in sight. "My heart has really skipped a beat, and I'm speechless upon seeing your gorgeous ass here," added Divine, while giving Hope a long, tight hug.

"You don't look too bad yourself, Mr. Divine," replied Hope.

"Where are all my single and independent sexy ladies at? Throw your hands up in the air to let that special one in the building know what time it," shouted the DJ over the microphone before playing "Slow Dance" by R. Kelly.

"Damn, baby, not "Slow Dance". You have to dance with me for our eleven-year anniversary," Divine said, as he pulled Hope to the dance floor.

As the liquor began to create a strong buzz within the bloodstream of the two, they discovered that the unbelievable chemistry they had already established years ago still remained. Hope began to rub and caress gently on Divine's back, as she looked him in his eyes. Then she gave him a peck on the lips before he held her closer to his body.

"Divine, I missed you."

"I miss a good woman like you more," Divine replied, as the two began to kiss.

Just then, Divine's phone started to vibrate, causing him to break his concentration and the kiss. As he removed his phone from its holster, he saw it was a text from Faith, which read, *I see your lips are occupied, which is probably why you have chosen to ignore my calls.* After reading this, Divine started to panic, knowing for sure that Faith was somewhere inside the club watching his every move.

Hope watched as Divine looked around nervously and asked, "Is everything okay?"

"Oh yeah," Divine replied, trying to compose himself. "Question is, are you okay?"

"Yes, I'm okay, but I do have to use the ladies' room," replied Hope.

"That's cool. I'll walk with you," Divine insisted, as they headed in the direction of the restrooms.

Man, where is this damn girl at? His question was soon answered when he looked up at the crowded stage to see Faith dancing with Danny Boy, but smiling wickedly at him. *Oh shit, I'm fucked.*

"Hope, can you hurry up because I'm not feeling well? My head is spinning and I need to get out of this club."

"Okay, baby, I'll hurry," Hope replied, as she rushed inside the restroom.

With her back toward Danny Boy, Faith sent Divine another text while she continued dancing. *I see you got some shit with you. You got too much on your plate for me. Enjoy yours, while I enjoy mine.* Having left Misty to be with Divine, who was treating her like the ex from her last male relationship, Faith felt like she had been hoodwinked.

"Are you ready to leave?" asked Hope, as she came out the restroom.

Damn, they're getting ready to leave, panicked Faith, after seeing the two walking towards the exit. She knew she had to think fast.

"My name is Faith. What's yours?" she asked Danny Boy, then slid her tongue down his neck.

"My name is Danny Boy, and I'm the birthday boy," replied the jovial and drunk Danny Boy.

"Oh yeah? Well, I got a cream-filled cake waiting for the birthday boy's candle to be placed in, if he's down," she whispered in his ear, while grabbing his hard anaconda.

"Oh, he's gonna put the candle in, and he just may eat all of the cake tonight," smiled Danny Boy.

"Come on. Let's go," Faith aggressively demanded, as she pulled Danny Boy's hand so she could rush to Divine, hoping to make him jealous.

Before Divine and Hope could exit the club, they were stopped by one of her friends, and Hope excused herself so her girlfriend could introduce her to her fiancé.

"Shit," grunted Divine, as he looked at Faith and Danny Boy approaching him.

"Hey, Divine," said Faith.

"Hey, Faith, how are you?" replied Divine, feeling discomfort with the situation.

"Oh, I'm well. I'm just really enjoying myself," she said.

Then, without warning, she turned and stopped a random guy walking by, and asked him to take a picture of them as she pulled out her camera.

Damn, thought Divine, as he looked at Danny Boy with a pissed-off expression, but Danny Boy was too busy looking Faith's body up and down to notice.

"Come on, guys," Faith said, as she stood in the middle of the two men with her drink in her hand.

Lord, please don't let Hope turn around, prayed Divine, as the guy snapped the picture.

"Do you want me to take a picture of you and your date?" asked Faith.

"No, we're okay. We were just about to leave," Divine responded.

After returning the camera to her purse, Faith spun around, and making it seem like an accident, she threw her Grey Goose and cranberry all over Divine's white outfit.

"Oh my God, I'm sorry! I've been drinking too much," Faith cried.

"Bit--" Divine said, catching himself before calling her out of her name. "It's okay," he quickly responded, as he noticed that Hope was still engrossed in the conversation she was having with her friend, and therefore, hadn't noticed what happened. "Danny Boy, go on and take her outta here. Enjoy yourself while she's wild, drunk, and ready," said Divine, giving his cousin a wink before he walked off with Faith.

"Oh, we're gonna have lots of fun. Aren't we?" Faith said, sucking in Danny Boy.

"My bad about the drink, cuz. Girl, come on," said Danny Boy, grabbing Faith's hand and dragging her off.

"It's alright. Everyone makes mistakes," Divine shouted out, as Hope turned around to see Divine's white clothes stained red.

"Divine, baby, what happened?"

"Just an accident, that's all. Are you ready? My clothes are soaked."

"Yeah, let's go and get you out of these wet clothes, and into something else that's wet," Hope replied, winking at him.

Deaubrey Devine

"That sounds good to me," responded Divine, even though he knew she wasn't serious since she was riding home with her friend, who had suddenly become Hope's designated driver.

Taking her hand, Divine guided her out of the club, with Hope's friend following closely behind with her fiancé.

CHAPTER 6

As Divine and Hope exited the club, Faith watched from the V.I.P. stage, knowing she had to shake Danny Boy, who she didn't want to be bothered with in the first place. Needless to say, Danny Boy had a few "not-so-nice" names to call her after she broke the news to him that she had only used him to make Divine jealous. Faith simply laughed at his obscenities, unmoved by his outburst, as she walked away to go hide behind the club's entrance, watching as Divine and Hope walked to the parking lot.

"Which car are you guys driving home?" asked Divine.

"We're taking my girl's car, and I'll stay the night over at her place. I'm going to leave my car parked here and just come back for it tomorrow since I'm in no condition to drive. Hold on, Divine," Hope said, as she stopped to bend down and take off her stilettos.

In the process of doing so, she dropped her rental car keys on the ground; however, Hope was too concerned with removing her corn-busting shoes to notice. And Divine was too busy watching her backside to realize it, either.

"Cute shoes, but they hurt," Hope commented, while holding the pumps in her hand. "Okay, sweetie, I'm ready," she said, as they resumed walking.

"I'll take these," said Faith to herself, as she snuck from behind the door undetected to pick up the car keys Hope dropped.

After making sure Hope made it to her friend's car safely, Divine texted Precious as he walked back to where his car was parked to see if she was going to come stay the night with him. While waiting on Precious' response, he received an unwelcome text from Faith.

All I need to know is if it's over. I deserve to know that so I can move on with my life, please.

Divine responded, *Haven't you already moved on with my cousin Danny Boy?*

It's obvious you don't know me. I'm not that type of woman to stoop that low and sleep with a family member. I just did that to make you jealous because you lied to me. I don't get down like that, replied Faith.

We're friends. Let's just keep it that way and not cross the line. You do you, and I'll do me, responded Divine.

Okay, I apologize for being a bother. You can text or call me when you want to talk. I see you're not ready for me. I think I'm starting to get the hint, replied Faith.

In between the back and forth messages of him and Faith, he received a text from Precious, who said she would meet him out front of his apartment.

Man, I'm getting tired of Faith and all her shit. I really need to settle down, thought Divine, as he started his car and pulled off.

A short time into his drive home, Divine called to check on Hope. "Are you feeling okay?"

"I feel much better now," Hope replied. "We stopped at a 24-hour drive-thru and I grabbed something to put on my stomach. Hopefully, this headache will go away after I get some rest. So where's the lucky lady?" she asked.

"I'm on the phone with her," replied Divine.

"Whatever, D, you've always been the ladies' man," laughed Hope.

"Naw, I'm single."

"Why?" Hope asked.

"Nowadays you never know who you're meeting. It seems like everyone is trying to come up off me with something negative and I'm trying to come up off them with something positive. I have friends, but they're all quantity and I need quality," responded Divine, trying to run game to let Hope know he was available.

Once again, Hope laughed. "You're crazy."

"What's up with you?" he asked, hoping she would respond by saying she was single, too.

"I'm in a crazy relationship with a sorry-ass loser that doesn't want to do anything but nickel and dime me. He talks like he's gonna go back to school to get his high school diploma, but stays posted in front of that stupid-ass Playstation, while I bust my ass to work and take care of the house. Some days, Divine, I just want to take that shit and burn it up. It works my nerves so bad," vented Hope.

"Damn, I didn't know you were into taking care of grown men," jabbed Divine, being sarcastic.

"I'm not. I just want to be there to help him get on his feet because he helped pay for me to get through school when he was selling drugs. The tables turned with our roles of taking care of each other when he got caught by the FEDS and did a few years time. Believe me; I don't plan on being here forever. I love him in a way, and it's just hard to turn your back on someone who has nothing now but were there for you when you didn't have anything," replied Hope.

"Don't be blind to people using you, though. The past is the past, and you grew up many years while he was locked down."

"Yeah, I know. Sad thing is not only is he not taking care of home, but he's not handling it in the bedroom, either. We only have sex every now and then."

"Well, at least you're having sex with someone," said Divine, playing like he was a born-again virgin.

"Boy, be quiet. I know someone's getting that good peter," Hope laughed.

"Girl, I wish. I'm about to explode from being overdue for a release," replied Divine.

"Well, one day I'm going to have to show you just how grown up I am," Hope giggled.

"So what's up with tonight? What are you doing?" asked Divine, hoping to pick up where they left off in the past.

"Boy, I'm almost in the bed at my friend's house. I may stop by for a few tomorrow before I leave for the airport. Okay?"

Damn, I thought I was going to get that tonight, thought Divine.

"Okay. Well, call me when you wake up. We probably can go out for breakfast if you're hungry and not hung over."

"Sounds good. Goodnight and pleasant dreams," responded Hope, ending the call.

Meanwhile as Divine was hanging up the phone with Hope, Precious was already waiting for him in her parked car outside of his apartment complex. Neal, who was on his way to Danny Boy's after party since he had already handled his business with his company that had left a short while ago, noticed Precious asleep with her head on the steering wheel and the window halfway down. Neal walked over to her car, reached in the window, and tapped her on the shoulder.

"Precious, are you okay?" Neal asked.

"Yeah, just a little tired," she replied, while rubbing her eyes. "Have you seen, Divine?"

"No, I was on my way to the after party. I have no idea where he is, but you're welcome to wait inside my apartment," Neal offered. "You shouldn't be sitting out here alone in your car with the windows rolled down like that."

"Oh, thank you," Precious replied, as she exited the car and Neal led the way.

"Would you like something to drink?" Neal asked once they were inside.

"Yes, some hot tea would be nice," she replied, as she stretched out on his couch.

When Neal returned with the tea, Precious suddenly felt a little uneasy being alone with Neal in his apartment.

"Look, Neal, I don't want to hold you up from attending the after party. I can wait in my car until Divine comes."

"You're more important. To be honest, I always had a lil thang for you, but you and my boy were talking a long time ago when we use to see you at the clubs," replied Neal, testing the waters to see how far he could go with her.

"Neal, stop playing. You're a trip," responded Precious, becoming more uneasy with the situation, and trying to think of how she could excuse herself from Neal's apartment without insulting him.

Meanwhile, Divine decided to call the redbone from the club that he saw dancing with the guy who had on the butterfly collar suit.

"Hello?" a female voice answered on the first ring, as if expecting his call.

"What's up, boo? What are you getting into tonight? By the way, I didn't get your name when I got the number."

"The name is Passion, and what will be up is you, if you're paying the right price," she responded.

"Damn, ma, I don't normally pay for it," responded Divine,

tripping out.

"Well, I don't normally give it away for free, but since you're so damn sexy, I might consider doing it this one time. In fact, maybe I can talk my friend who I strip with to come along with me."

"Well, bring y'all asses on then," Divine replied, ready to get the show on and popping. "Do you guys smoke weed?"

"Hell yeah. You got bud?" Passion asked.

"Yeah, so write down this address," said Divine, as he gave her the directions to his apartment.

After hanging up with Passion, Divine sent Precious a text informing her that he would be going to his cousin's after party instead of meeting her at his place. Afterwards, he placed a call to Neal.

Just as the text came through on Precious' phone, Neal's phone rang.

"Neal, meet me at my apartment for a prayer meeting and a freaky show with the redbone from the club. She's even bringing her stripper friend," said Divine.

"Man, I'm chilling with my friend from out of town. I'll have to miss out on this one," Neal replied.

"Oh well, more for me to enjoy. I'll see you later," said Divine, as he continued driving to his apartment.

"Who was that?" Precious asked after Neal hung up.

"Nobody," smiled Neal innocently.

"Neal, please be upfront with me." Precious already had a gut feeling it was Divine.

"That was Divine. He asked me did I want to join him with some girls that he just met in the club. I told him no and that I was chilling with my company. I would rather hang with you, and that's real shit, Precious," Neal said, hoping he had increased his chances of getting some from the fine-figured woman in his presence.

"Oh, hell naw! Let me call his fuckin' ass," Precious said, while starting to dial Divine's number.

"No, don't do that," Neal said, grabbing her hand to prevent her from placing the call. "Just know that Divine is a hoe, and pretend like the fly on the wall never said anything," winked Neal, as he looked her in the eyes.

"I guess you're right," replied Precious, as she allowed Neal to begin kissing her while in a hurt and vulnerable state of mind.

As the two began to make out, with Neal removing her clothes and whispering promises of taking their secret to his grave, Divine was next door hitting a blunt and the skins of the two dancers who were doing any and everything sexually imaginable to him and to each other. Needless to say, they kept Divine mesmerized with their sexual skills throughout the night. So much so that Divine didn't think twice about stopping the freak session to attend his cousin's after party.

Hell, I can see that nigga anytime. I'm going to stay my ass right here and party like it's my birthday, Divine said to himself.

Meanwhile, Faith sat in her car, fuming. As she watched the last of the people leave the club, she thought to herself, *All men are the same...dogs.* Twisted thoughts of the love and hate she had for Divine continued to play through her mind. Looking over at Hope's keys she had placed in the passenger's seat, she suddenly got an idea.

Exiting her car, she pushed the alarm button until she heard Hope's car go off. Since there were only a few cars remaining in the lot, which probably belonged to the management and staff of the club, it was not hard at all to spot it. Hopping inside Hope's car, Faith pealed out of the lot.

CHAPTER 7

The next morning after sending Passion and her freak friend on their way, Divine busied himself with cleaning up around his apartment, while listening to a church service being broadcasted over the radio. He suddenly started reminiscing back to when his mother and father would take him to church each and every Sunday, and then like a ton a bricks, it hit him just how much he had fallen off course in his life. He knew they were probably turning over in their graves with disappointment in the man he had turned into, and he became very somber with the thought. Just then, his phone rang, jarring him from his thoughts.

"Divine, I'm sorry to bother you, but I need a huge favor," Faith said when he answered.

Divine frowned up his face with anger before asking, "What's up?"

"Well, I believe I lost my credit card somewhere in the club last night, and when I went back to check, they didn't find it. My Nextel corporate phone bill needs to be paid before tomorrow, or else they will disconnect my phone, and I can't have that. I would ask my mother to do it for me, but she doesn't have a credit card. You know how older people can be with credit. They rather pay in cash then risk destroying their credit or accruing the interest on plastic. But if you could please do me the favor of paying my bill with your credit card, I'll give you the money now before I go to catch my flight home," Faith said pleadingly.

Divine didn't know if he was just a sucker or if the church music playing in the background softened his heart enough for him to show some compassion to Faith and her situation. Whichever it was he gave in to her request. "Okay, bring the money over, and I'll pay it for you," responded Divine out of kindness.

"Thanks, friend," Faith replied, as Divine hung up the phone so he could continue cleaning up.

When the pastor on the radio began his sermon, Divine had the feeling that he was speaking directly to him, with his references to fornication, infidelity, and other sins that result with one's weakness to the temptation of the flesh. That's when Divine started to think about Precious and Danny Boy, who were both married but cheating on their mates. Then he thought about the numerous women he had slept with, including his one-night stand with Faith and his most recent sexual escapade with the two strippers who had left his place that morning. The more he thought about the reckless way that he was living, and how that was not the type of man his parents had raised him to be, the more he felt a desire to change his ways.

A few hours passed, and Faith arrived. When she called to let him know she was there, he decided to go out to her car instead of having her come into his apartment and not be able to get rid of her.

"Thank you so much, D," she said, as she handed Divine one hundred dollars and her billing statement which contained her account information through her open window.

"You're welcome," Divine replied.

"So, what are your plans for the day?" Faith asked, attempting to spark up a conversation, while glancing up at his door to see what his apartment number was since clearly it wasn't the one she thought, but instead Neal's apartment number. However, when she looked, she found it was missing.

"Well, the 'boss' is going to church," he said.

"Boss, eh? Boss of what?" she laughed. "Anywho, that's a turn-on for a guy to be saved," responded Faith.

"Okay," Divine said, not interested in what did or did not turn her on. His only interest was in getting rid of her. "Well, I'm going to talk to you another time. I need to go get ready. I'll take care of this for you a little later on today," he added, as he began to walk away.

"Alrighty, I guess I'll just call you when I get back to Houston."

"Okay," responded Divine, as he picked up his pace to get away from her as quickly as possible.

There's a lily in the valley bright as the morning star.

"Aw, man, this use to be my favorite song to wake up to on Sunday mornings. I love Pastor John P. Kee's music," Divine said, as made up his mind to get ready and visit the church down the road from where he lived.

Shortly after showering and dressing, he received a call from Hope.

"Did you move my car last night, Divine?" asked Hope in a puzzled voice.

"No. What happened to your car?" responded Divine, sounding just as puzzled by her question.

"I must have dropped my keys last night, and someone moved my car from where I parked it. It was only around the corner, but I thought you may have been playing one of your little high-school tricks that you were once famous for doing," replied Hope.

"Well did you find your keys?" asked Divine.

"Yes, someone turned them into the club owner."

"See, you need to stop drinking like that," chuckled Divine.

"Shut up. I hear your gospel music in the background. That's good that you listen to the Sunday morning show, but are you going to church this morning, my brother?" questioned Hope, trying to see where Divine's head was at.

"Why, yes, I am. If I can go out to the club on Saturday, I can get up and give the Lord some time on Sunday," replied Divine in a prestigious scholar voice.

"I hear ya. That's what I need to be doing myself."

"Well, you're welcome to come with me if you want," Divine said, extending an invitation.

"I would love to, D, but I need to get my things together to leave. But, a sistah will treat a brotha out to lunch after service, if that's okay."

"Sounds like a plan. I'll call you after service lets out."

"Alright, don't forget to call me," Hope replied.

"Believe me, I won't. I think I need this date as a refresher," giggled Divine, as he said goodbye and headed out to church.

When Divine arrived at church, he felt a little awkward since he hadn't been going to church except for on Easter Sunday, Christmas, and New Year's Eve, and he had found no church home. Divine sat in the back so no one would bother him in the small church, and just as the pastor's wife stood up to do the announcement, Divine exited the church for the restroom with his index finger in the air so he wouldn't have to stand up and introduce himself as a visitor. When he returned to his seat and heard the pastor preaching the sermon on deliverance, he started to feel like he was being held back and bound by all the women, parties, and drugs. Divine felt in his heart that he wanted a new start, and God really couldn't bless him if He wasn't inside of him. After service, Divine returned home so he could change into something more comfortable for his lunch date with Hope.

When Hope called to tell Divine she had arrived, he went outside to get in her car.

"Damn, girl, you look even better than you did last night," smiled Divine.

"And just what does that mean? I hope that's a good thing, because I was tore up last night." Hope replied.

"All I'm saying is you look damn good, and I like your hair."

Hope gave him a flattering look. "Thank you. I rushed to my girl's shop to get it done this morning before I go back to Connecticut. I haven't found anyone up there that does it like her. That's one of the reasons why I miss home in the ATL."

"Well, that should be one of the reasons why you move back," Divine replied, as they both began to laugh.

"I wish, but I have a good job up there as a loan officer."

"Dang, at least consider it as an option if you and your boyfriend don't work out," Divine replied, as Hope blushed with a warm smile. "I know that's the biggest reason why you moved to his hometown after you finished high school anyway. You were in love with the older dope boy that flashed the shiny things at the young tenderoni and took you away from me. Wow!" expressed Divine, letting Hope know how he felt.

"Well, Divine, sometimes you do strange things when you're young and in love," she responded, knowing that Divine was telling the truth and that she deserved a guy like him in her life, but was instead stuck with her boyfriend who she couldn't just leave in peace without him snapping and trying to hurt the both of them. "I'll keep moving back here as an option, though. Now let's go get something to eat."

By the time they finished having brunch, they had caught up on a majority of things that had happened in each other's lives during their ten-year absence from one another.

"I wish we could start all over" Divine stated, as Hope smiled and her eyes filled with tears.

"Divine, I hear you, but just remember that it will take us both to put forth the effort to get to know each other and work toward being friends or whatever role God has planned for us to be in each other's lives."

"I feel ya. I just want you to know you're special to me, and I don't want to get hurt or hurt you," Divine replied, while wiping away the single tear that fell from Hope's left eye.

Divine as he squeezed Hope's hand harder as he looked at a tear fall from Hope's left eye.

"Thank you. Just pray for our situations," she said, as she grabbed his hand with hers and held it tight.

"Yes, and let's plan to get together and hangout sometime in the near future. If we don't plan, it won't happen," Divine replied.

"I agree," she said, as they prepared to leave the restaurant so Hope could drop him off back at his apartment and make it in time to catch her flight home.

Later that day, Divine dressed to attend the church revival across town that they had announced during service that morning.

As Divine sat in the back under the tent, where he was being bitten by mosquitoes mercilessly, he clapped along while the choir sang. While clapping, he noticed a beautiful slanted-eyed woman in the choir singing to the top of her lungs. As the dark, royal chocolate woman sang, Divine couldn't take his eyes off her; he felt himself attracted to her spiritually. Even after the choir finished their selection and the pastor had gotten up to preach, Divine was distracted by the woman's beauty.

Lord, I know I'm not supposed to come to church to try and meet women, but please forgive me as I step to this beautiful woman after service.

By the time the preacher finished his sermon, Divine had made up in his mind that he was going to give his life to God. When the pastor called the congregation down to the front, the woman who had him mesmerized took a little girl by the hand and walked down to the altar with another woman, as Divine quickly followed to stand at the altar next to the women.

When the preacher came to Divine to pray for him, lay his hands upon him, and ask did he confess with his mouth that Jesus died on the cross to save our sins, Divine replied, "Yes, thank you, Jesus!" as the spirit hit him, and he lifted his hands and started crying. Divine felt like a huge burden had been lifted off of his heart.

Next, the attractive woman's friend received the Holy Spirit and had a shouting session of her own before passing out for a short time on the ground.

After returning to his seat, Divine quickly looked around in hopes of seeing the black beauty and introducing himself to her after the revival concluded. However, he didn't see her anywhere in sight. After scanning the whole perimeter, Divine thought, *Oh well, I have to charge that to the game, but dang that girl was right.*

Disappointed that he had let that one slip away, he returned home so he could get some rest before going into work that night.

"Whaddup, Divine? I haven't seen you all day," Neal said when Divine arrived at work. Neal attempted to strike up a conversation in hopes of fending off the guilty conscience he was feeling after having had sex with Precious. "What's been up with you, Mr. Incognito?"

"Man, I went to church," replied Divine.

Neal laughed. "Nigga, stop lying."

"For real, and I also went to a revival that was held earlier this evening."

"Man, what has gotten into you? Did you wake up to red lipstick on the bathroom mirror from Faith who told you she had AIDS or something?" harassed Neal.

"Hell naw, bro. I wouldn't be here right now if that had happen. I'd be in jail for killing her," responded Divine, while Neal laughed at his response. "Man, I just feel refreshed, like I'm new," he described.

"Well, speaking of new. I have this new green from my homeboy for a nice celebration of you feeling rejuvenated, and we can both be on cloud nine in the prayer meeting when you roll this up," Neal said, as he produced an ounce of marijuana.

"Neal, the only prayer meeting I'm gonna have from now on is the one that's for God. I'm gonna have to retire from the blunt and get right," replied Divine, making a life changing decision.

His friend looked at him like he was crazy. "What? Man, you are really buggin', talking about you're gonna retire from the hydro. Dude, you're trippin' hard. I'll respect you, though," responded Neal.

Well, you don't mind me hitting the joint, do ya?"

"Nope, go right ahead, my brother. The preacher just preached about we all have our time and place of deliverance. I don't want you to change because of me."

"Man, come on, D. Some preachers even hit the joint. That's why a preacher can't tell me anything. If you don't know a word, where do you look, Divine?"

"You would look in dictionary," replied Divine to the crazy question Neal asked him.

"Exactly my point! It doesn't take a rocket scientist to figure that out. What the hell do I look like going to church to give a pastor all my damn money so they can get rich?" said Neal, as he rolled up a blunt and started to smoke. "You sure you're retired?" he asked, as he started to feel the slow motion and stoned feeling.

"Yeah, bitch, now leave me alone before I relapse," laughed Divine, who was trying to avoid the temptation with all of his might.

"Nigga, you look like a relapse and a recap," Neal howled with laughter.

"Lord, forgive me for cursing," Divine said, as he started the nightshift with Neal.

Deaubrey Devine

CHAPTER 8

"Divine, did you get a chance to pay my cell phone bill?" asked Faith, when she called him the next day.

"Yes, ma'am. I paid it with my credit card and got you all squared away."

"Thanks so much," replied Faith. "So how was church yesterday?"

"It was nice, refreshing. I even attended a revival last night and gave my life to God," Divine quickly responded, hoping his revelation would run Faith off, but no such luck.

"That's nice to hear. I did that a few years ago and backslid, but I need you to pray for me," replied Faith in a carefree manner.

"I will. We have to pray for each other," Divine said, as he thought back to when they were intimate on the cruise. "Let me ask you something, Faith. "Do you normally have sex on the first night with random guys you meet?"

"No, Divine. I'm not a slut, if that's what you're asking. I just felt you for some reason and wanted to make love to you. Never in life did I think about having sex on that trip," responded Faith, but Divine was not a believer. "I really miss you, and have been wondering why I'm so in love with you. I always think about laying my head on your chest as we looked at the stars," Faith said, hoping Divine would give her feedback for his change in actions.

"It was just a great moment. Maybe we can relive that moment one day with our significant other," Divine replied nonchalantly, while throwing a hint about them not having sex again.

"What do you think about long distant relationships?" asked Faith, totally ignoring his last statement.

"They're okay, but I can't really get into them because I'm an

58

affectionate person when it comes to time with my mate," replied Divine, as he began to think about Hope. "For instance, I have a friend that was at the party who I wanted to spend a little more time with, but she lives in another state," admitted Divine, letting Faith know he was interested in someone else.

"Oh yeah?" Faith replied, as she started glowing on the inside, thinking that Divine was talking about her. "Well, she needs to make a move to be with her future then, huh?" Faith said, throwing a hint.

Divine giggled, while still thinking about Hope. "Yeah, I just wish it was that easy," he wearily added out of longing.

"You never know. It could happen sooner than you think. By the way, I sent you the picture we took at the party. I think you looked very handsome…well, before I spilled my drink on you, that is."

"Don't even remind me of that bullshit," responded Divine, becoming pissed off again.

"I'm sorry. It was an accident."

"Okay, well, thanks for sending it. I'll talk to you a little later. I'm going to go run a few errands," Divine said, using that as an excuse to end their call.

"I'll be waiting," she responded right before hanging up.

Divine exhaled deeply, and once again wondered how he had gotten himself so deeply involved with Faith, who should have been nothing more than a one-night stand.

Not long after Divine got off the phone with Faith, Cherish called to see if he would be interested in attending church with her that evening since he had shared with her his desire to find a church home. Not having any plans for the evening, he accepted his cousin's invitation.

When Divine arrived at the church, Cherish was pulling up behind him in her car. After getting out and hugging each other, they walked up to the church together. When Divine opened the door for his cousin, he began to bob his head to the singing of the choir.

"Dang, Cherish, now I like this," Divine said as the music overtook his body, soul, and spirit.

The whole congregation was standing, as the choir director led the song of worship. Most were moved to lift their hands and cry out to God.

As Divine looked around at everyone, he took notice of a few females. "Cuz, there are some hoes up in here," he commented, whispering in Cherish's ear.

"Boy, watch your mouth and stop calling women that. Focus on God," replied Cherish as she began to sing the worship song.

As Divine looked at the choir in the front of the church, he noticed the beautiful chocolate Barbie from the revival tent singing to the top of her lungs with her arms stretched high above her. At that moment, Divine fell instantly in love with the woman's spirit and love she displayed for God. He knew if she had that same love for a mate as she had for God, she would give her all in a relationship.

After they finished singing, the pastor told the choir members they could leave out the choir stand to make room for the guest choir. As the choir members exited out the side door, Divine never took his eyes off the woman.

Damn, should I get up to go catch her or should I just keep visiting with Cherish and maybe I'll run into her sometime at church?

Divine didn't have to think too long about what to do, because while the tithes were being taken up, a woman came up to him.

"Excuse me," a soft voice said, and as he looked up, he saw the beauty from the choir and her friend asking could they get by to take a seat in the pew.

"Hey, Destiny, come on and sit down, girl," Cherish said, making room for her friend.

Thank you, Lord, thought Divine, as he moved his legs to the side to let the women slide through.

While the other choir sang and the pastor preached, Divine looked out the corner of his eye the whole time to scan the woman up and down, while taking in Destiny's beauty. After the conclusion of the church service, Divine was introduced to Destiny by Cherish, and the two shook hands, with Divine looking at her left hand to see if it had a wedding ring on it.

Destiny smiled extra hard before turning to Cherish. "Alright, Cherish, I'll talk with you later. I have to go pick up my daughter from the church's daycare."

"Okay, Destiny," replied Cherish.

As Destiny walked off, Divine waited patiently to get the 411 on the woman from his cousin.

"And before you even start annoying me about hooking you up, Destiny is single and looking for a good Christian man to help her and be a dad for her daughter. She doesn't need a player or have time for games," stated Cherish to nip all the foolishness in the bud.

"Dang, Cherish, that's the old me. I'll call you later," smirked Divine, as he darted off. "Excuse me, where is the daycare?" Divine asked a passing usher.

When Divine reached his destination and saw Destiny, he wasted no time in stepping to her.

"Hello again, Destiny. I don't mean to bother you or step to you in a disrespectful way, but I think you're a gorgeous woman and I really loved the way you worshiped God earlier in the choir stand," said Divine, as Destiny thanked him. "I saw you at the revival the other night, and I must say that I thought I would never see you again. I just couldn't let the opportunity to get to know you slip by me twice."

"I saw you, also," Destiny stated, while smiling. "That's funny, because I looked at you like *dang, he's so sexy*. It's rare to find a young black male in church these days."

"Well, I must admit going to service on my own is new to me. It used to be that my mother had to pull me by the ear to make me come to church."

Destiny giggled. "You're crazy," she responded.

"Mommy, I'm hungry," her daughter said, interrupting the conversation.

"Aww, lil' momma is so precious," complimented Divine, as he reached out to shake the girl's hand.

"Oh my God, Desire is never friendly to those who she doesn't know," replied a shocked Destiny, as she watched her daughter be cordial to Divine.

"Maybe it's God brewing up something," hinted Divine, as they both laughed. "Well, I don't mean to hold you up. I just needed to meet a good-hearted church woman to have as a friend in my life."

"Okay, it was nice meeting you," replied Destiny, blushing.

I'm going to wait until Sunday to get the digits. I don't want to appear desperate, thought Divine.

As Destiny watched him turn and walk away, she thought, *Dang, he's not even going to ask me for my number.*

"Divine!" yelled Destiny as he turned around. "Did you forget to ask me for something?"

Divine started smiling. "I think I did," he replied, as Destiny reached in her purse for a pen and piece of paper.

"Call me," Destiny said, handing him over the piece of paper with her number written on it.

Yes, thought Divine from scoring big time and getting her number, as he walked away for the second time.

On Divine's way to work, he received a text from Faith, which read: *After the party on Saturday night, I wish we could have hung out. I just wanted to hug your neck. I think about you a lot and hate sweat'n you. We were one on the cruise, and now it's whatever. I'm sorry for venting, but I'm just hurt.*

Whatever, said Divine to himself after reading the text. Instead of responding to Faith's message, he decided to text "hello" to Hope and then called Destiny after he had started his shift and while Neal took his routine nap.

"So what's up? Why are you single?" Divine asked Destiny after she answered.

"I'm single because I refuse to settle any longer. I'm tired of being hurt, toyed with, and taken for granted. I don't want to be single. I truly believe my husband is out there somewhere. I'm ready for the man that is so in love with me that he will do anything, and I will feel and do the same," she replied.

"Just so you know I feel the exact same way. It's tough and sad for me, but it's real. Maybe it will happen soon," Divine expressed. "You know, sometimes I just want to serve God a little more and give a little more towards the kingdom," he added.

"Maybe you should consider joining the church choir," suggested Destiny.

"I really can't sing worth a lick. I sing in the shower, but ya'll are way too much for me," replied Divine.

"It's singing for the Lord. You can just blend in," Destiny explained. "Rehearsal is on Thursday nights at seven o'clock. You should come out tomorrow."

"I may," Divine said, and then they continued to talk for a while longer before ending the conversation, with him once again telling her he would consider coming to choir rehearsal the next evening.

When Divine got off the phone with Destiny, he received a call from Precious, who was crying.

"What's wrong?" Divine asked out of concern.

"I want to tell you something before Neal does," sobbed Precious. "I'm so sorry, Divine."

"What's up, boo? Talk to me," said Divine in a comforting voice, while looking over at Neal who was sleep with his head on the desk.

"The night of Danny Boy's party, when you lied to me about meeting me at your apartment and you had those girls over, I was next door at Neal's apartment feeling neglected, horny, hurt, and sick. After Neal told me that you wanted him to join you with some girls on some freak-type shit, I was crushed. He then went on to tell me about how much of a hoe you are, and for me to not say anything to you about what he told me. The whole time he used my vulnerable and hurt state to get inside my mind and pants," Precious revealed.

"What?" snapped Divine, wanting to punch Neal, who was still sleeping, in the back of the head for the disrespect he had shown their friendship by doing such a thing. After taking a few deep breaths and calming down, he continued. "Look, Precious, we needed to stop all that anyway," he said, while thinking about the sin he was committing by being sexually involved with her. "I'm sorry for disrespecting you and your husband. I'm blown and can't believe you gave away my benefits, but I'm cool."

"I'm sorry. My feelings were just as destroyed when I heard that. So, I guess I did it out of revenge," replied Precious.

"Look, let's just move on from it and drop it. I won't let Neal know you told me. You're good. I'm okay with just ending what we've had. If we ever feel the need to call and check on how the other is doing, we know each other's numbers. Take care," said Divine, and then quickly hung up before Precious could say another word.

As he thought about all that he and Neal had been through as homeboys, he found out that little loyalty laid between homies and being between a woman's thighs.

"What's up, Mr. Pastor?" asked Neal the next morning as they walked to clock out.

"Nothing, bro. Just pray for me as I pray for you," replied Divine, not letting on that he knew anything about what had happened between Neal and Precious, but thinking to himself, *I'll be a damn fool to bring another girl around your ass.*

CHAPTER 9

Dang, I shouldn't have come this early, Divine thought, having arrived thirty-five minutes early only to have to sit and wait for the choir rehearsal to start.

As the director and different members began to arrive, Destiny came up to Divine and said, "Hey, sorry I'm running a little late. I had to pick Desire up from daycare."

"You're alright, but you better hurry and get up there in the choir stand. I think the director is calling everyone for prayer," Divine said right before Destiny rushed off to join them.

After the rehearsal, the director came up to Divine. "Hello, my name is Director Dawn. Are you interested in becoming a member of the choir?"

"Yes, I've never experienced anyone pray like that in my life, and the way everything went at rehearsal today makes me definitely want to be a part of the choir," replied Divine.

"I'm glad God could use me to bless your life. Just come here tomorrow morning at ten o'clock with a song to sing, and we'll place you in the correct group you need to be singing in."

"I have to audition for a spot in the choir? I can't sing that well," Divine said, as if preparing the director of his vocal capability, "but I'll be here."

As Divine was telling Director Dawn he would see her tomorrow, Destiny walked up. "Hey, Director, I see you've met Divine," she said, while smiling and giving Director Dawn the eye, as if to say, *Girl, do you see this fine brother I've came across.*

Director Dawn smiled back at her. "Yes, Destiny, I have met Divine. He's set to meet me tomorrow to be placed in a certain section so he can sit out his three services and then join the choir to sing with you," she explained.

"Alright, Divine, you have to blow her away tomorrow to get a lead role," said Destiny.

Divine laughed. "Yeah right, I'll be lucky to get in the choir with my rooster-like voice."

"You'll do well. It's not that serious. Remember, it's for God. He'll take control if you take one step forward," Director Dawn replied. as she smiled to encourage Divine. "Okay, I'll let you guys talk. I have a long day tomorrow. Bye, Destiny. Bye, Desire," Director Dawn said, while bending over to hug Desire. "Bye, Divine. It was nice meeting you," she said, as she stuck out her hand to shake Divine's hand before departing.

As the three walked to Destiny's car, Desire reached out to take hold of Divine's hand. Touched by Desire's willingness to reach out to him, he slightly raised both of their hands so Destiny could take notice of the two holding hands.

"Do you want to have any more children?" Divine asked.

"No, she's more than enough for me. How about you?"

"Well, yes, I would like to have a few when I marry, especially since I don't have any yet," Divine replied.

Although he was disappointed with her response, he wasn't going to back down with pursuing her, thinking that if they got close enough he could persuade her to change her mind in the future.

When they reached the car, Destiny strapped Desire into her car seat, then turned to Divine and said, "Thanks for walking us to the car."

"The pleasure was all mine," replied Divine, as the thought of him being with one woman instead of messing around with numerous women like some type of gigolo crossed his mind.

While Destiny was looking at Divine with a beautiful smile that showed her sparkling white teeth, his male hormones took over and he inched pulled Destiny closer. With her squeezing Divine's neck a little tighter, she closed her eyes and the two started to kiss, sending chills all over their bodies from the sensation. Desire simply looked on with a huge grin on her face. After a minute or so, Destiny pulled back a little as she exhaled.

"Boy, let me stop before I put something on you right here on these church premises. It's been a minute for me," Destiny revealed.

"Wow, you're a great kisser," Divine responded in awe.

"Naw, you got me. You're the one with the sweet tongue," described Destiny, as they both chuckled. "Let me go ahead and get to the house so I can put Desire to bed and get my clothes together for our anniversary picnic tomorrow. I have to be on my feet all day and help as one of the servers."

"Well, call me when you get settled," he said.

On the way back to his apartment, Divine called his Uncle Earl to make sure everything was a go as far as him working with his uncle, who was starting a cleaning service in three weeks.

Meanwhile, on the other side of town, Cherish called Destiny to ask if she had a pair of running shoes she could borrow because she left hers in Divine's trunk.

"I don't have any, but why don't you just go over to Divine's apartment to get them?" asked Destiny.

"I don't know. He may have company, and I don't want to intrude," replied Cherish.

"I doubt he has company. I just saw him at choir rehearsal. I tell you what...I'll go over there if you watch Desire and give me directions," Destiny quickly responded.

Cherish laughed. "Your grown behind just wants to see Divine."

"Girl, he's trying to holla, and I'm kinda feeling him. I need to see what company he may have over this time of night," said Destiny, acting as her own private investigator.

"Well, come on and drop off Desire. But let me call this boy before he trips because you just popped up over there."

After Cherish called to inform Divine that Destiny was coming over to get her tennis shoes for her, Divine rushed around to clean up and take a quick shower before her arrival. Just in case something went down between them, he wanted to make sure he was his freshest.

When Destiny rang the doorbell, Divine had not long ago finished his shower. So, he simply threw on a pair of jeans and answered the door with beads of water still on his chest.

"Dang, Divine, you're even sexier with no shirt on. Look at you with muscles everywhere," Destiny said, while entering.

"I'm sorry for answering the door like this. I was trying to unwind and chill for a minute before I hit the sack, when Cherish called," replied Divine, playing off the timing up of his plot.

"No need to apologize, boo. You look very tempting."

"Alright now, I already want to make love to you. You better chill with all that," expressed Divine, exposing his feelings for Destiny. "Well, let me go put on some clothes," he said, as Destiny took a seat on the couch.

"You're okay," she replied, quickly jumping up and walking over to him.

When she reached him, she wrapped her arms around his neck and began kissing him. The soft kiss soon turned intense right along with Divine's growing bulge.

"Woo, Divine, that's full grown," Destiny commented, feeling it press into the side of her rib cage.

"What's up? Feel that and see how hard it is," commanded Divine, while dropping his jeans to his ankles and stepping out of them.

"Damn, you have a big-ass dick," Destiny said, as she took it in her hand and began to play with it by squeezing it. "What are you going to do with this?" probed Destiny. "Do you have protection?"

"Yes, the extra thin kind," replied Divine, as he took her hand and walked her back to his room where she started to get undressed.

As Destiny waited in the bed, Divine looked in his bottom dresser drawer to find out that he didn't have any more condoms.

"Damn!" shouted Divine in disbelief.

"Don't tell me you don't have any condoms."

"I do. Hold on," Divine said, as he rushed to the living room to retrieve the spare condoms he kept underneath the cushion of his sofa.

When he returned to the bedroom, Destiny was standing with her pants in her hands. "I thought you didn't have protection."

"I do, darling. Look," Divine replied, shaking the pack of condoms in the air before placing them on the nightstand. "Come here," he said, gently pulling Destiny toward him as he began to kiss on her neck.

With Divine's kisses taking a journey all over Destiny's ears, neck, and body, the temperature in the room started to skyrocket, and it became hard for them to contain their desire for one another. As Divine sucked on her breast and then went lower to start kissing the sides of Destiny's stomach, she squirmed from the pleasurable feeling.

Exploring further below, Divine placed his whole mouth around Destiny's pussy lips and softly sucked before letting his tongue penetrate deeply inside. He began to wiggle his muscular organ around a little before he licked her from the bottom to the top. While mistreating Destiny's clitoris with his tongue, moving it back and forth like a rattlesnake's rattler, he looked up as Destiny inhaled and exhaled deeply.

"No, baby, I can't take this," Destiny said, pushing his head away. She didn't want him to stop but she couldn't take the indescribable pleasure.

"Baby, I want you to relax for me," whispered Divine.

"I'm sorry. It's just been so long for me," replied Destiny, as her legs started shaking.

"It's been a long time for me, as well," Divine lied. "Let's just enjoy the moment," he said, as he allowed his lips to caress and draw all of Destiny's juices into his mouth.

"Damn, baby, I've never had this done to me before like this. No one has ever made me cum once, and you've already made me have multiple orgasms," Destiny moaned, going crazy from releasing.

"I want you to have as many orgasms as you can handle," he responded, then turned her over on all fours in the doggy style position.

As he continued licking her from behind, Destiny's body continued to tremble from the mini orgasms she was experiencing.

"Oh, Divine, I've never had anyone make my body feel like this before," she moaned, while gripping the sheets. "This is some out-of-this-planet shit the way you're making me feel."

"I wanna make you feel like this every day," Divine said, before flipping her over onto her back again.

Destiny watched as Divine struggled for a minute with sliding the condom on.

"You are too big for that condom. You may need to get a few Magnums the next time," laughed Destiny.

To silence her, he kissed her fully on the lips, while scooting her body further up in the bed so they could assume the missionary position. As Divine eased inside Destiny, she made noises and squirmed, trying to adjust her walls to the girth of his penis.

"Hold on, baby, go slow," coached Destiny, as she pushed Divine's stomach back and slightly pulled away from him. "It's been a long time, Divine," she added, letting him know to take it easy and not be impatient.

Man, fuck, thought Divine as he looked down to see that he had softened due to her breaking his concentration and the mood.

"Did you cum?"

"Naw, baby, I'm just tripping right now," replied Divine.

"What's wrong? You're not attracted to me?" asked Destiny.

"Oh no, babe, it's not that. My body's just a little tired from working out earlier."

"Well, I want you to get yours, so take the condom off and let me see what I can do to help."

Divine smiled as he laid back on the bed. After straddling the lower part of his legs, Destiny took his manhood in her hand and began to repeatedly twirl it while looking closely at it.

"What are you doing?" asked Divine.

"I have to examine it," replied Destiny, snickering.

"Boo, the dick is safe. Go on and do your thing."

"Don't get mad at me. I haven't gone down on a guy in years. And please don't come in my mouth." Destiny felt very uncomfortable going down on Divine, but at the same time she wanted to please him as he had pleased her.

"I won't. It's okay. Just try it," Divine replied, growing impatient.

"Alright, here we go," said Destiny, as if giving herself a prep talk.

She started off slow, but soon increased the pace. As she sucked his dick out of control, Divine bounced up and down on the bed like he was riding a damn bull at a rodeo show.

"Damn, baby, you got this piece right. Come here," said Divine, his heading spinning.

With his penis now hard again, he laid her on her back to make love to her until he exploded.

As soon as Destiny went in the bathroom to freshen up before leaving, Divine kneeled on the side of the bed and silently prayed, *Lord, please forgive me for sleeping with her. I need major help with my weakness when it comes to females and sex.*

When Destiny called to say she had made it home safely, Divine apologized for his actions, feeling a deep sense of guilt.

"No need to apologize. We were two consenting adults. I don't know about you, but I was long overdue. You see how you had me shaking," laughed Destiny.

"I know. It looked like you were having a seizure. It kind of scared me," teased Divine.

"Shut up," she said, as she continued to laugh.

"Seriously, though, I'm just into you for some reason and I barely know you," responded Divine.

"I know. It's kind of scaring me," Destiny admitted.

"Well, sometimes you have to give someone a chance, and then love like you've never been hurt before," said Divine, imparting knowledge into Destiny's head.

"You have some very deep words. Do you rehearse what you will say to women?"

"No, these are not rehearsed words. I'm speaking from the depth of my heart. I've wanted to share my heart with someone for a while, and I feel you may be just the one I can do that with," Divine responded.

"Okay, I feel you on that. By the way, I'm glad you stayed up and waited on me to get home. The bombs I've talked to in the past would have gone to bed after I left their house."

"Well, that's one of the many differences between a man and a boy," boasted Divine, hoping to get kudos for his actions.

"Before we hang up, can you honestly tell me how many partners have you been with before and did you practice safe sex with each of them? There are so many diseases going around these days, and I think this is a topic that many people fail to discuss. I get checked regularly, but to make the both of us more comfortable, I just want to know since all of this has happened so quick," said Destiny.

"Suga, I've protected myself very well, with the exception of a few serious relationships I was in. Look, how about we both go get tested so we will know for sure that we're not bringing any diseases to one another? Let's just make time to go get tested together," said Divine after sensing the nervousness in Destiny's voice.

"Well, go ahead and make yourself an appointment, and I'll do the same. We both work different schedules, so we'll have to test separately. Alright, well, have a good day tomorrow, and may the good Lord give you as many blessings with your singing for Director Dawn as he has given me since I've met you a few days ago."

"Thank you, sweetie," Divine replied, as they ended the call.

As he laid down to go to sleep, thoughts of Hope crossed his mind. Although his heart was still with Hope, he had to accept the fact that she was still in love with her man. Therefore, he would have to fill that empty void by growing closer to Destiny and creating a steady relationship with someone who was near and who he could spend the quality time that he desired to spend with someone special.

CHAPTER 10

*Jesus is real…I know. The Lord is real to m*e… sang Divine Friday morning, as he prepared to go tryout for the church choir. Right in the middle of the chorus, his phone rang, and it was Hope.

"Hey, handsome, how are you? Haven't talked to you in a while and wanted to check up on you."

"I'm fine. I was just getting ready to walk out the door in a few minutes. I'm auditioning for the choir at my cousin's church. Wish me luck. God knows I'll need it."

Hope giggled. "I'm sure you'll do just fine. I wish this boyfriend of mine was a God-fearing man. Last night, we argued so much, I had to take some Tylenol for my headache," Hope sighed. "But I want you to know that I appreciate your friendship through all this, Divine. I have a lot going on, and I'm just trying to find an easy way to exit out of this relationship without all the drama."

"Well, you're in a crazy situation and God is the only person that can give you direction on that situation. Just pray about it. But, hey, I hate to cut this conversation short, but I must really get going so I won't be late."

"I understand," Hope replied. "Good luck, and blow their ears off. I'll talk with you later."

No sooner than he had hung up with Hope, Destiny called.

"Good morning, Divine. I was thinking about you while getting Desire ready for daycare, and wanted to call and wish you luck."

"Aww, thank you, and please kiss Desire for me," replied Divine.

"Will do. Make sure you call and let me know how it goes. Okay?"

"I'll be sure to hit you later," Divine said, as he ended the call and left out the door, while thinking his morning couldn't get any better since he had heard from the two most important women in his life.

While Divine and another woman waited in the church's office lobby for an older gentleman to finish auditioning with Director Dawn, he received a text message from Faith, which read, *You haven't returned any of my texts or calls. Did you get the pictures from Danny Boy's party?"*

Not yet, he simply replied.

So what's up? Why haven't I heard from you? If you would rather I stop calling and texting you, just let me know. However, I was hoping to see you this weekend since I'm off.

Growing annoyed with her persistent behavior, Divine responded, *Faith, I'm going to be honest with you. I have a steady friend, and I'm gonna try to be a one-woman guy. We can still be friends as long as you respect what I'm trying to do.*

Faith's heart dropped at this news. *I kind of sensed that,* she texted. *Don't understand why you didn't tell me that and be upfront, though. I really don't know what to say right now, so I'll talk to you later.*

Divine felt somewhat guilty for not having cut it off with Faith early on, but he knew there was nothing he could do to change the past. Just then, Director Dawn jarred him from his thoughts by calling him into her office to audition.

While Divine was behind Director Dawn's closed doors singing his heart out, Faith sat seething and wanting revenge for the pain he had caused her. The first thing she thought of was to hit him where it would hurt: his pockets. So, with eyes filled with tears, she placed a call to Nextel and made a payment towards her bill with Divine's credit card number that she remembered had been saved on file from the last time he paid it for her.

Hell, he owes me, she thought as she completed the transaction.

Afterwards, she went over to Misty's house to completely break it off with her. Faith expressed her desire to be with Divine, and told Misty of her plans to move from Houston to Atlanta in order to do so.

"You're a slimy, confused-ass bitch," responded Misty out of hurt.

"Baby, please don't talk to me that way. I thought at one point I was done with men, but I'm actually not. I actually think I love him."

"Bitch, you met him in a fucking casino. You don't even know him, and you're talking about moving to be closer to him. You have to be friends before anything else, or have you already crossed that line with him?" asked Misty, as Faith began to cry.

"Misty, I've thought a lot about what it would be like to be without you over the last month or so. I dig you and will miss you much, but I want a child someday and don't want my child to be confused or teased by his or her classmates in school for having two mommies. I want a man like the bible says I should have," explained Faith.

"What the fuck am I suppose to do when you leave? You're not thinking about me. You act like your feelings are the only ones that matter. I'm tired of you bouncing back and forth between being with men and being with me. This is not a damn tennis match!"

"Alright, enough with all the belittling. I just need to move on so I can heal from this relationship. I'll be moving very soon. Please, Misty, don't be upset with me. I'll always care for you," Faith replied, as she went over to hug Misty, who held her head down and refused to look Faith in the eyes.

"I understand. Do your thang. Just remember, a man can't lick you like a woman can!" Misty called out as Faith departed.

As Faith was leaving Misty's house in Houston, Divine was walking through the office doors to meet with his boss, who had called and said he needed to see him as soon as possible.

"Come in and have a seat," his boss said.

As Divine took a seat, he wondered what was the reason for him being called into the boss's office.

"Divine, were you really sick the week that you missed work and called off a few hours before you were supposed to come in?"

"Yes, sir, I was," replied Divine with a straight face.

"Well, this mail that was addressed Attention: Boss, but also has your name on it shows otherwise," his boss said, while handing over an envelope that contained the card and pictures Faith had sent. "I thought it was something concerning the business of this security firm since it was addressed "Boss", and that's why I opened it."

Divine was heated. *How could her ass be so careless as to send some shit like this to my job,* he thought as he read the short message she had written inside the card.

I'm sorry for spilling my drink on your clothes. Danny Boy told me how you worked hard to tell your boss that you were sick just so you could call off and attend his party. Then I go and ruin your night by being clumsy. I hope these pictures will make up for my accident, and remind you of how sexy you looked before my little mishap.

Love always, Faith.

After reading the message, Divine looked up at his boss, speechless.

"Well, is there anything you have to say?" his boss asked.

"No, sir," replied Divine, knowing he had been busted.

"Divine, if you wanted to attend your cousin's event, all you had to do was be upfront and say you needed off. Since you're still on probation because you were clocking Neal in and out when he was at work, I'm afraid I'm going to have to let you go."

Divine panicked at the thought of being without work until his Uncle Earl started up the cleaning business, which wouldn't be for another three weeks at the least.

"Boss, this is the only job I have right now. Can I have a few extra weeks until I find something else?" asked Divine, hoping his boss would have some sympathy.

"No, Divine. You should have thought about the consequences before you made some of your irresponsible decisions. As of now, you're terminated and you'll receive a letter in the mail."

"Okay, Sir. Thank you for allowing me to work at the complex," Divine said, feeling defeated.

"By the way, your discount for rent will also be terminated immediately," he added.

"Okay," replied Divine, as he thought *that stupid bitch Faith,* while heading out of the office.

Livid, Divine placed a call to Faith. When she saw his name pop up on her Caller ID, she was so excited.

"Hey, honey. Did you get the card?" asked Faith, thinking he was calling to thank her for being so thoughtful.

"Hell yeah, I got the card and a pink slip to go along with it. Those fucking pictures cost me my damn job! Why in the hell did you address it to "The Boss" instead of putting my name on the envelope?

Better yet, why didn't you just mail it directly do my apartment instead of my job?" questioned Divine with an attitude.

"Oh my, I'm sorry. I don't know your apartment number because that bit of information is missing from your door, so I decided just to send it to the security office so you could have a surprise at your job from a special someone. And I addressed it to "The Boss" because of the one time when you boasted about being the boss jokingly. I sincerely didn't mean for it to cause you any problems on your job."

"Faith, look, I need to know what your intentions are for you and me. And please be honest," Divine said, getting straight to the point.

"I want to try and make it work between us no matter how long it takes," Faith replied bluntly.

"But I told you before that we could only be friends because I'm dating someone now. So, please, let's just be friends and not come at each other any kind of way. I know we already crossed the line, but let's just let that be in the past."

"You can't just cross the line and then forget it ever happened," Faith replied. "Besides, I'm supposed to move to Atlanta at the first of the month, which is in a few weeks. I've applied for two jobs with mortgage firms there and have an interview set up. I already have my real estate agent license to work in both states because I lived in Atlanta for a few months when I first graduated from college years ago. Seeing as though I don't know anyone there, you'll have to show a friend around," Faith divulged, giving Divine insight on her situation.

Man, what the hell, Divine thought. "Why Atlanta? You don't have relatives here, do you?" he responded, shocked by her announcement.

"Well, the real estate industry there is very hot right now, and this one particular firm has offered me a job with great benefits, extra incentives, and a chance to come up off extra bonus money," Faith said with excitement.

"Well, holla at me when you get here, but promise that you'll respect my relationship," Divine replied, hoping to dissolve their intimate relationship but still salvage a friendship.

"I will, and thanks, Divine. Once again, I'm sorry about your job," she said before ending their call.

CHAPTER 11

"Why haven't I heard from you today, Mr. Man?" asked Destiny, when she called Divine early that evening.

"I had a long, bad day. I lost my job," he replied in a depressed tone.

"Oh crap. I'm sorry to hear that, but you know God takes you from glory to glory and elevates you when things happen. So, don't worry about that old job. Just get ready for a better job," responded Destiny to encourage Divine.

Dang, this is what I need in my life, Divine thought, as he felt drawn a little closer to Destiny with her wise words.

"So how did you lose your job?"

"It's a long story, and I really don't want to talk about it now," responded Divine.

"Well, I miss you, if that helps put a smile on your face," she said, attempting to lift Divine's spirits.

"The feeling is mutual. I've been thinking of you a lot today, also."

"So how did the audition with Director Dawn go? Do I have a new choir buddy to sing along with?" asked Destiny enthusiastically.

"It went well. That was one of the only bright points of my day," replied Divine, as Destiny shouted with joy at the news that he had made the choir. "So are you visiting me today?"

"Yep, Cherish is going to watch Desire for me, and I can stay the night if you want me to," Destiny replied.

"That's cool," Divine said, as he began to perk up a bit at the thought of seeing her later.

"In celebration of your acceptance into the choir, I cooked a special dinner for you tonight. I prayed on it and felt it in my heart that you would do well, and since you're a single man, I figured you would welcome having a home cooked meal. Therefore, I'm bringing dinner to you instead of us going out to eat. I'm going southern style on you. I fixed meatloaf, greens, black-eyed peas, dirty rice, macaroni and cheese, and cornbread. For dessert, I fixed your favorite: carrot cake. How's that sound?"

"Sounds like I need someone like you in my presence to brighten up my dark day right now," Divine replied, while licking his lips and thinking about the meal he would soon be devouring. "By the way, how did you know that carrot cake is my favorite?"

"Oh, let's just say I have a way of finding out what a person who is special to me likes," replied Destiny, as she thought, *Thank you, Cherish, for hooking a sistah up with the info.*

"So what time will you be over so I can eat all this good food you're bragging about?"

"I'll be on my way so your taste buds won't have to wait any longer," she said, and then they ended their call with promises of seeing each other in a short while.

Just then, there was loud knocking at Divine's door.

"Who is it?" he called out.

"It's your cuzzo. Open up," Danny Boy responded from the other side.

"Damn, cuz, what's up? I have company on their way," Divine said, while swinging open the door.

"Man, I won't stay long. Fix me a splash. And what bitch you got coming over now?" asked Danny Boy, thinking Divine had one of his playthings dropping by.

"Cuz, this ain't no bitch. You should see her. This damn girl is tight," replied Divine, bragging while fixing Danny Boy a Grey Goose and cranberry. "This girl just might be the one."

"Oh shit, nigga. Here you go with this 'she may be the one' shit again. D, you be falling in love with the pussy too quick. You think that every girl that puts the ass on you is the right one or The One. Nigga, chill out and be patient," responded Danny Boy, who was growing tired of hearing about the love life of the freelancing Divine.

"Whatever. I think this girl may be the one for real. She's tight and I met her in church, not a club, nigga," responded Divine, as they heard a knock at the door.

"Sit down, bitch, and act sociable," Divine said, as he smoothed the wrinkles from his shirt, patted his hair, and did the breath test by blowing into his hand.

Danny Boy laughed. "Man, cut all that shit out and open the door."

"Who is it?" Divine asked.

"It's the person you've been expecting," replied the sweet voice, as Divine opened the door and hugged Destiny, who held some plastic bags in her hands.

"It sure is. Hey, sunshine. Dang, baby, let me get those bags for you. My wife's not going to carry no bags around me," Divine said, as he took the bags from her.

"I'm sorry, Divine. I didn't know you had company. Hello," she said, speaking to Danny Boy.

"Oh, lil momma, I was just stopping through for a minute."

"I'm Destiny by the way," she replied, as she extended her hand to give Danny Boy a handshake.

"It's a pleasure to meet you. I'm Danny Boy, Divine's cousin. I've heard a lot about you, and it's good to finally put a face to the name."

"It's nice to meet you, as well. Divine, I have your food in the car on the back seat," she said, while turning to face him. "Could you go out and get it, please?"

"Of course, baby. Come on, cuz. You can walk with me and to your car," Divine said, implying that it was time for Danny Boy to break out.

"Once again, it was a pleasure meeting you," Danny Boy told Destiny before following Divine out the door.

"So what's up? What do you think about her body?" Divine asked as they walked toward the parking lot.

"Cuz, she's tight. She seems to be a good look, but just chill with her nigga. I see your ass already love the girl," responded Danny Boy.

"I wouldn't say that I love her yet, but I do love our conversations about some real stuff. I'm just tired of all these games and different women. I really just want to settle down and start a family," craved Divine.

"Shit, nigga, you just talking. You ain't ready for all that responsibility. But, she seems to be a damn good catch, D. Just treat her right and see what she's talking about," Danny Boy suggested, as he continued on to his car.

Divine stood carefully considering the words his cousin had spoken, as Danny Boy beeped his horn and pulled off.

"Thanks, baby, for the food. It was very thoughtful of you, and I really appreciate it," Divine said after they finished eating.

"I just wanted to thank you for taking another step where God wants you to be," smiled Destiny.

"I needed to see my lil suga to sweeten up my day," said Divine, as he walked around the table to hug Destiny from behind. "Thanks for your friendship," he added before leaning around and kissing her on the lips.

"Come on," Destiny said, while jumping up from her seat. "Let's go take a shower and wash away the stress from the day."

After pulling Divine to the bathroom, she adjusted the water for the shower and then removed his shirt, while the two kissed with an intense passion.

"Dang, you waste no time, huh?" Destiny commented, observing the rise in Divine's jeans right before he dropped them to his feet.

While Divine was stepping out of them, Destiny stripped her clothes from her body in lightening speed.

"You have me going crazy like this, with your sexy ass," replied Divine, while standing naked in the steamy bathroom.

"Boy, I thought about you all night, and woke up wet this morning. And that's not normal for me. Come on, let's get in," Destiny urged, as she pulled back the shower curtain so they could step inside.

After Divine was positioned in front of the hot water, he applied a generous amount of body wash to a body sponge and instructed Destiny to turn around so he could lather up her back.

"See, that's how stuff gets started," warned Divine as he reached under Destiny's left arm to grab her breast. "Why are you pushing this soft booty all up on me like that? You know it arouses me to the max," said Divine, while sliding the sponge down her body to her wet juice box.

After Destiny turned around and reached up to pull the showerhead down so her hair wouldn't get wet, she locked tongues with Divine for a few seconds before taking the sponge from him to add soap and indulgently lather up his body.

"Sweetie, go ahead and rinse off," she then said.

As the water bounced off Divine's muscular shoulder blades and splashed Destiny in her face, she closed her eyes and giggled.

"Oh, Divine, my hair is getting wet!" she shouted, while raising her hands to try and block the water from wetting her hair.

"Oh shoot, my bad," laughed Divine.

Taken in by the well-developed cuts of Divine's body, she began rubbing all over him to help remove the soap residue. After all traces of the body wash had been washed away, they switched places and Divine returned the favor of exploring her with his hands to remove any soap that had been left behind on her curvaceous body.

"By the way, I want my engagement present from you to be some breast implants," hinted Destiny as Divine laughed. "I'm serious. Shoot, I can't have Desire having more than me when she gets a few years older," giggled Destiny.

"Girl, hush and relax," whispered Divine, while lifting her leg to rest on the edge of the tub so he could slid up in her from behind.

"Yes, baby. Please be my king!" shouted Destiny, as she leaned over and balanced herself by placing her hands on the edges of the tub.

"Only if you'll be my queen," Divine responded, penetrating her deeper and deeper with each thrust, as the erotic emotions began to heighten along with the temperature from the hot shower.

"I am, baby. I wanna be your queen!" yelled Destiny.

Not having used a condom, the two were taking a major risk. Divine, however, did act responsibly when it came time for him to erupt, and pulled out right as he exploded on her back.

"That was a great shower, Divine," declared Destiny after they had washed each other for a second time.

With a smile upon her face, she cuddled in Divine's arms and they fell asleep listening to slow music from the MP3 player on Divine's cell phone.

CHAPTER 12

"Baby, thanks for a pleasurable night," Destiny said, before departing the next morning.

"No, thank you for being the one to make it pleasurable," Divine replied while walking her to the door. "Please make sure you call me after you get home and settled after picking up Desire."

After planting a soft kiss goodbye upon his lips, Destiny said, "I'll be sure to do that. Talk to you soon."

After watching Destiny walk to her car, Divine turned to grab the mail from out of his mailbox, then went inside and shut the door behind him.

"Bills, bills, bills," Divine said, flipping through the envelopes. *I have to come up with a plan. Geesh, my lights are schedule to be turned off soon and my refrigerator is damn near bare,* he thought, as he took a seat at the kitchen table and started to write down payment methods of how he would pay his bills until he started working with his uncle.

After he came up with a plan to pay his bills, created a really tight budget for the next month, and wrote out checks for the current bills due, he went outside just in time to catch the mailman before he pulled off from delivering mail to the different apartment complexes. With only a few dollars remaining in his pocket, Divine decided to go to the store to get some much-needed groceries.

"Damn, come on car," said Divine as he attempted to turn the switch over, but it wouldn't start.

The extremely irritated Divine tried several more times before calling his uncle Earl, who brought over the family mechanic.

"Are you sure the head is cracked?" asked Divine, hoping that wasn't the case.

"Yes, the engine is gone," the mechanic informed him. "It would actually cost just as much to buy another car than to replace the engine and pay for the labor."

Divine hung his head not knowing what to do.

"Well, you need a reliable car, Divine, so just call my car dealer and see if he can work something out for you," suggested Uncle Earl, as he handed Divine a business card out of his wallet and then called to leave a message for his friend on his office voicemail.

After returning home from getting a few groceries from the convenience store down the street, he noticed he had a message from the car dealer, and returned his call to let him know he would be down to the dealership the next morning. As Divine sat reflecting on the fact that he had no job, no car, and no money, Destiny called to invite him to join her and Desire for an outing in the park. After he told her the news about his car, she assured him that she didn't have a problem coming to pick him up.

An hour later, Destiny arrived.

"Hey, Desire," Divine said, as he placed his beach towel and small book bag that held his portable DVD player and old comforter in the back seat next to her.

"Helwhoa," Desire replied, waving with excitement.

Nervously, Destiny observed how Divine would react to her child, who had a slight speech problem. However, she saw no change in his facial expression that indicated he was uncomfortable with her daughter's problem with speech. Deep inside, though, Divine was questioning whether he was ready for the possibility of becoming a stepfather to Desire.

After they were on their way to the park, Destiny decided to ask a burning question that had been on her mind for a while. "Divine, are you looking to settle down? I mean, you know, have a serious, committed relationship?"

As Divine sat with an uncomfortable look upon his face, Destiny felt the need to apologize. "I'm sorry. I hope I didn't scare you with my question. I'm just curious, that's all."

"Destiny, I'm digging you out of control," Divine finally replied, choosing his words carefully, "but I don't want to rush or classify our friendship now with a 'girlfriend-boyfriend' label. I think we need a little time to get to know each other. Now let me ask you a question."

"Yes?" Destiny said, as she took her eyes off the road for a split

Deaubrey Devine

second to look over at him.

"What was up with that strange look you gave me when I spoke to Desire? You probably didn't think I noticed, but I did."

"I'm sorry. I get kind of protective when it comes to Desire because of her speech problem. Just don't want my baby to be mistreated or picked on by people because of it."

"Destiny, you do not have to worry about me being one of those people. You have a gift from God, and through prayer, He will bless her with the ability to be able to perform at a high level and achieve better than many scholars through the prayer that will be placed on her life. We all are made different in our own special way. I can sit down with Desire and have her repeat sound words after me and engage her in activities to help her speech," he added, causing Destiny to experience a feeling of relief with knowing he accepted her daughter.

After arriving at the park a few minutes later and walking to a nice, spacious area, Divine spread out the comforter, while taking in the beautiful sunny day, with its slight breeze and clear blue skies. They then put on a DVD cartoon to watch as they laid down to eat fruit snacks, chips, and drinks from the goodie bags Destiny had prepared for their outing.

As they spent good quality family time together, Divine held Desire close to him, as she snuggled her little four-year-old body against his chest. Destiny took that moment to thank God for bringing a man into her life that not only cared about her, but her daughter, as well.

A few hours after Destiny dropped Divine off at his apartment that evening, he tried calling Destiny from his cell phone, only to find that it had been disconnected for non-payment.

Damn, thought Divine as he sat disgusted by the fact that he had no way of communicating with Destiny. He thought about going next door to Neal's apartment to borrow his phone to call Destiny, but thought about how he needed to stay away from his backstabbing homeboy and the temptation of indulging in a prayer meeting.

While he was sitting at the house bored, Lemon Head knocked on the door.

"Dang, girl, I haven't seen you in a minute. How have you been?" asked Divine after opening the door and letting her inside.

"I've been okay. Just a little busy going in and out of town with my job as a flight attendant. You see, though, when I come in town, I haven't forgotten about ya. I'll never leave ya nor forsake ya. Now move so I can get me a lil cup of something," she said as she walked over to the liquor cabinet and poured herself a glass of gin before returning to the couch. "So what's new, superstar?" asked Lemon Head.

"Girl, I have some good news and bad news," responded Divine.

"What's the bad news first?"

"Man, I've lost my damn job, the engine went on my car, my cell phone is disconnected, and I'm broke," replied Divine, slamming his friend with his pity party.

"Damn!" yelled Lemon Head, as she jumped up and began rolling her sexy belly around. "Don't tell me that I'm gonna have to start working all this sexiness to get my superstar straight."

"Girl, sit your crazy behind down. I'll be okay because the good news is that I'm saved now," Divine divulged, while Lemon Head raised her eyebrows in surprise.

"You're what?" she asked in disbelief, as Divine confirmed that he gave his life to God and joined the choir.

"Damn, Divine," Lemon Head said, as she folded her arms and poked out her bottom lip. "You were supposed to let me put it on your sexy ass one more time before you went and did something like that. Now I don't feel right playing with you, pastor."

"I'm okay. You can even stay the night if you want," invited Divine, who wanted to test his commitment of being saved and possessing self-control of not being able to sleep around freely.

"Okay, sounds good to me. I don't have any other plans for tonight."

After they talked for a few hours and Lemon Head had a few more drinks, they went to the bedroom, where Divine climbed under the sheets with his boxers on and immediately turned away from Lemon Head so he wouldn't be tempted to hold or touch her.

Lord, I need your strength, Divine silently prayed, trying to maintain the willpower to ignore her nude body lying next to him.

"Damn, Divine, is everything alright?" she asked, feeling his tension. "I don't want to make you uncomfortable."

"I'm alright. I was just thinking of some things," replied Divine, as he turned to face her in the bed. "There is someone I recently met."

"Really?" Lemon Head asked. However, she had no interest in hearing Divine speak about other females. Still, being a friend, she feigned an interest in what he had to say.

"Her name is Destiny, and we met at church. It seems like I grew feelings for her instantly. It's like one of those relationships in the beginning where you meet a new person and want to stay on the phone all night. You constantly think about that person all damn day, and can't wait until you see them again," Divine expressed, feeling much joy inside.

"Dang, Divine, I see you have some deep feelings for this chick," responded Lemon Head.

"Yeah, I have a strong desire to get to know her so that we can move forward to a relationship someday," expressed Divine.

"Well, I understand that, but where does that leave us?"

"I don't really know. All I do know is that we may need to chill on the sex tip," justified Divine.

"You know what, Divine? I'm not even mad at you. I'll respect you and her, but if you guys ever split up, just know that I'm here for ya and I'll still put it on ya like we just met," laughed Lemon Head, as Divine snuggled with her before falling asleep.

CHAPTER 13

The next morning, Destiny popped up over Divine's place to give him a ride to church as he showered to get ready for his uncle Earl to come pick him up so they could go to the car dealership. The thoughtful Destiny went to go pick him up out of concern when she couldn't reach him by phone because it had been disconnected.

"Hey," Lemon Head said, greeting Destiny at the door. "You must be Destiny. Divine has told me all about you. Girl, how are you?" asked Lemon Head, as she extended her hand to shake Destiny's.

"Who are you?" inquired Destiny, with a strange expression on her face.

"I'm Lemon Head, Divine's godsister. That's what I was nicknamed, because as a child, I use to love the sour taste of lemons. Come on in. I was just finishing up cooking for Divine," she explained, as Destiny followed her into the kitchen. "I try to cook for Divine every now and then so he can have a good meal instead of microwave dinners all the time. So do you like, Divine? He told me about church and how he feels you a lot. He needs a good woman to keep him in line."

The gullible Destiny smiled upon hearing this. "Girl, I think Divine is a good catch. Knock on wood," she said, while tapping her knuckles on the kitchen table.

As Divine entered the kitchen, he silently prayed Lemon Head had not said anything stupid.

"Divine, your future wife is very sweet," commented Lemon Head, smiling.

"Hey, Divine," Destiny said, while standing. "I apologize for dropping by unannounced, but when I tried to call, I learned your phone was off. I came by to see if you needed a ride to church since you are without a car right now."

"Yeah, I forgot to pay the bill," replied Divine, as Lemon Head gathered her keys and walked toward the door.

"Hey, you guys go ahead and talk. I have to go meet my boyfriend so we can go to church. It was a pleasure meeting you, Destiny, and I'll call you later, Divine. Oh my bad, I can't do that," laughed Lemon Head.

"Oh hush," Divine replied before she left out of the apartment. "I'm glad you came," he said, turning his attention back to Destiny. "I was going with my uncle to go check out a car this morning, but I'll tell him we can go tomorrow. May I use your phone to let him know of the change in plans?"

After placing the call to his uncle Earl, he changed into his Sunday's best attire, and the two left out the front door.

During the service, the pastor preached on the importance of tithing. *If you give your tithe of ten percent, God will bless it to come back to you pressed down, shaken together, and running over the top. Don't be afraid to be a giver. Step out on faith and give, even if it's your last,* he heard the pastor say, as he began to think about his bills, which were accumulating.

Lord, please bless me, Divine prayed, as he put his last in the collection plate while it was being passed by.

As he listened to the pastor preach about wisdom, knowledge, and understanding from the book of Proverbs, he took notes so that he could use them later for his uplifting bible studies he did at home. After the service, Divine filled out a prayer request and dropped it in the prayer box. He certainly needed all the prayers he could get to help him get through all that he was currently going through.

The next day, Divine and Uncle Earl went to the car dealership. As the dealer looked over some paperwork, he asked Divine if he could put down $1,500.

"I don't have that kind of money, but I need a car to get around. Is there any way you can do it with no money down?" negotiated Divine.

"No, I'm afraid not. You have to put something down. Can you write a postdated check that we can hold until you tell us to cash it?"

asked the dealer.

"Yes, I'll postdate it for a month from now."

"Unfortunately, we can only take a check dated fifteen days out from today's date," the dealer informed him.

Left with no other choice, Divine postdated the check for the maximum time allowable per the dealership's policy, signed the paperwork, and drove off the lot in his new car. Afterwards, Divine ran to pay off a few past-due utility notices he had received in the mail. He prayed the checks he had just written out wouldn't clear his bank until after his last check with the security firm was deposited directly into his account, which would hopefully be in the next day or two. Upon returning home, Divine focused on the sermon from the day before and positioned himself a little closer to God by praying despite his many shortcomings.

Wednesday night, Divine attended church and once again took notes from the pastor's sermon and filled out another prayer request. After church, he turned down Destiny's offer to come over to his place because he just wasn't in the mood for company.

The next morning, Divine used the business center in the apartment complex's lobby so he could go online and check his bank account to see how much was deposited into his account from his paycheck. Upon signing in, he noticed he had a negative balance as a result of the checks clearing before his paycheck was actually deposited. Thinking quickly, he remembered an advertisement he had seen listed in the local paper about a junkyard that paid cash for junk cars, and even hauled them away free of charge. Not hesitating, he called and arranged for them to pick up his old car, for which they offered him four hundred dollars in cash. Immediately upon receiving the cash, he rushed to the bank to deposit the money into his account, which barely covered the funds his bank paid out and the overdraft fees.

With everything seeming like it was going wrong for him, Divine immediately fell into a state of depression and removed himself from everyone and everything. As the days passed, Divine stayed within the confines of his apartment, and ignored the calls and knocks at his door from Neal, Danny Boy, Uncle Earl, Cherish, and Destiny, who came over to check on him since no one had heard from him lately.

After coming down with a 24-hour virus, Divine woke up Sunday morning feeling weak and not having the desire to go to church.

However, he thought back on the time that he found his blessing, which was Destiny, received the awesome Word, and joined a church. So, he dressed and found the strength to attend. That Sunday would be his third sit-out, which meant he would officially be allowed to sing in the choir during Wednesday's service. Once he arrived at church, he searched for Destiny's face in the choir, but she had stayed at home, upset and hurt, thinking Divine had broken things off with her. Outside the church, Cherish caught up with Divine before he could get in his car and leave.

"Divine, where have you been? Everyone has been worried sick about you, including Destiny, who calls me constantly to find out if I've heard anything from you."

"I apologize. Just pray for your cuz. I've been going through some things that only God can handle," replied Divine.

"Well, just go on through it, not just to it," laughed Cherish. "By the way, my dad has been trying to get in touch with you, as well. He's been concerned about you."

"I'll make it a point to give him a call later," said Divine, as he jumped in his car and headed home.

Wednesday evening, as he lip synched the songs he didn't know, he realized the atmosphere and the anointing in the choir stand was powerful as his heart raced with passion. After the pastor released the choir to go sit in the congregation, Divine went up to Destiny in the hallway to apologize for being so distant.

"Divine, please don't say anything to me," Destiny said in a hostile attitude, as she walked past him and went to sit next to her aunt.

After church, Divine tried to approach Destiny again when she was picking up Desire from the church's daycare.

"Hello, Destiny. Hey, Desire!" Divine said.

When Desire smiled and reached out for him, Destiny snatched her child back.

"Divine, are you slow and not getting the picture? I said don't say anything to me, and that means my child, also. Go take your lil player games to those hood rats and chicken heads, because I don't have time for them. I'm not a clip note or magazine story that you can keep reverting back to for the same thing. It's just not going to work out between us. So, let's just be honest and face the truth," exploded

Destiny before walking away.

What's up with her? thought Divine, ignoring the red flags of Destiny's mood disorder.

Later that night, Divine listened to his gospel music and prayed for vision and deliverance. As a result of him keeping the faith, he didn't have to wait long for an answer to his prayers. That Saturday morning, God spoke to his spirit and told him to check his bank account. After going to the business center, he logged on to his online banking and discovered he was $1,000 in the plus as a result of his former boss depositing his sick days and holiday pay into his account.

"Thank you, Lord. You're a provider. You make a way out of no way," Divine cried with joy.

The financial setback and hardships he had been through in the past few weeks humbled Divine, and it was at that moment that he realized the Lord was just starting his work through him.

CHAPTER 14

"Hello," Destiny said, answering her phone curtly the next morning.

"Hey, Destiny, how have you been?" asked Divine in a calm voice, happy to hear her voice.

"Hey, what's up? Everything's been kosher over here on this end, pimp," replied Destiny sarcastically.

"I've been thinking of you. I miss seeing your smile," expressed Divine, hoping to penetrate a layer beneath her rudeness.

"Look, Divine, we're both grown. I don't want to play with you and don't want you playing with me. I don't just want to lay up with you because I'm old fashion when it comes to that. I'm in need of longevity with a little blingy and not shacking up. Besides, what do you really want and need from little ole me?" asked Destiny, cutting straight to the point.

"What are you talking about?" responded Divine in a state of confusion.

"Divine, over the last few days I've been thinking about what type of guy I'm really getting involved with. On one hand, you seem to be the perfect catch, but on the other, you've been avoiding me when the only thing I was trying to do was check on you and be in your corner," vented Destiny.

"Destiny, I've just been experiencing a run in with God, as he has been showing things through shaping and molding me to how he wants me to be. I'm sorry. I promise I haven't been messing around or creeping. I've just been witnessing God work miracles before my eyes. Have you ever cheated or been cheated on?" asked Divine, as Destiny ignored the question. "Well, I guess I should only assume my own answers to my question since you're not talking to me," said Divine.

"Yes, I have cheated before and I'm very sensible to little games," replied Destiny in shame.

"Well, I have, also, and it's not a pleasant feeling. I'm not going to mess it up with you by trying to gamester with other women. I want us to understand one another and be on the same page from here on out," responded Divine, sharing his valley experiences with Destiny, who began to lighten up upon hearing this.

"Are you sure you haven't been creeping?" inquired Destiny, while smiling on the inside.

"No, baby, I'm being honest on that one," replied Divine. "So, would you like to go on a date tonight?" he asked, hoping they could make up for missed quality time.

"Hold on for a second. Let me see if I have a sitter," she said, as she put down the phone to go ask her aunt, whom she lived with, if she would mind watching Desire for a few hours. "I would love to go out," Destiny said when she returned to the phone.

"Cool. I'll be there to pick you up around eight o'clock. How's that sound?"

"Sounds like a date. I'll see you then."

Approaching Destiny's house, he called to let her know he was driving down her street. When he pulled up in the driveway, Destiny rushed outside.

"Dang, do you live with a guy? Are you trying to time things so you won't get caught up?"

"No, my aunt is just nosey. I'll be glad when I move out and get my own apartment so I can get away from her. She's a piece of work, but she's a great baby sitter," smiled Destiny as Divine pulled off. "I'm sorry for tripping earlier. I'm just starting to care about you a lot."

"I care for you, also. I often think of you, and really think that in time, we'll have something special," replied Divine, while Destiny looked at him with a sad expression.

"I know this may sound crazy, but I really need a guy like you. I hope you're not playing games with my emotions," Destiny said, exposing her feelings.

Wanting her to know that he was just as serious about her as she was for him, Divine pulled the car to the curb, reached over, and gave her a hug.

"We'll continue to get to know each other, and it will work with both of us working together. Just know that I need a woman of God like you, also, and I'm in your corner. Pray for us," he replied, then kissed her softly on the check before continuing to drive to the movie theater.

When they arrived, Divine asked Destiny what movie she would like to see.

"It doesn't matter. I want you to take control and pick out the movie," she replied.

"You're cool. Just tell me what type of movie you like."

"Look, Divine, I can't make all the decisions for us if we ever get together. Now you go ahead and pick a movie, or we can go do something else," snapped Destiny.

What the hell? All this attitude about picking a movie? She can't be serious. Man, this is a serious turn off. I'm out when we get back, thought Divine, while looking up on the board to select a movie. *Maybe she just needs a little structure and discipline in her life.*

He decided on a comedy, paid for two tickets, and then they walked to the concession stand to get a large popcorn and soda. Once inside the movie, the two shared an evening of laughs.

After Divine dropped Destiny off, he returned home and decided to wash the few dishes that were in his sink. While doing so, his phone rang, and he quickly dried his hands on a dish towel so he could answer it.

"Hello," answered Divine.

"Hello, stranger. Dang, what did I do to you? Wow, I mean I can't even get a 'Hey, how you doing? How your momma and them doing?'" joked Hope, as Divine laughed.

"Baby, stop tripping," responded Divine, as he continued to giggle from Hope's sense of humor.

"Oh, that's funny? That's okay, Divine. Go ahead and laugh at me. It's cool," poured on Hope, as Divine snickered.

"Stop acting like that, silly. So what's been up? I've been thinking of you."

"Divine, if you were that concerned and thinking of me, you would have called to check up on me," replied Hope to his game.

"I apologize, but my phone was disconnected for a minute," explained Divine.

"I kind of figured that or that you changed your number after I tried to call and couldn't reach you. Dang, you could have had Danny Boy tell me or something. I thought my conversations had bored you."

"Never that. You're my jewel that I have to keep close to my heart," smiled Divine.

"Awww, you made me smile just now," replied Hope.

"So what's up with you?" Divine asked.

"Nothing really. My body is ready for a 'Calgon, take me away' moment. I just came back from doing some cardio and yoga at the fitness center. I'm feeling pretty good right now," replied the lively Hope.

"So I know your man can't wait to oil and massage that smooth silky skin down," hinted Divine.

"Don't even bring his sorry ass up," she replied in a pissed off tone.

"Why did you say that?"

"D, this guy is beginning to send me through some bullshit. First of all, he's on probation for a disorderly conduct charge he caught at a spade game with his family, when he went off acting like a damn nut on them with his bad attitude. Secondly, he tried me today. He asked me to give him a ride to these Saturday meetings he has to attend in order to avoid jail time for violating his probation. I was trying to be nice by giving him a ride using my high-priced gas, but then when we were pulling up to the building, this sorry cornball asked me for money for his restitution that he needs to pay every time he attends these meetings. Divine, I looked at his ass like he was crazy and thought to myself, '*You're nothing but a sorry, lazy-ass nigga*'. I went ahead and gave him the money just so I could get him out of my face and so he wouldn't throw up in my face how he took care of me before getting knocked. I'm so ready for a change. I'm almost on the verge of having a nervous breakdown. I'm tired of being up at three and four in the morning arguing over stupid shit and being called everything but a child of God."

Deaubrey Devine

"Well, he's going to continue to take advantage of your kindness until you make a move to get rid of him," replied Divine.

"I wish it was that easy, but when he leaves, he comes back and tries to fight my little guy friends. He has even got into it with a police officer that asked him to leave before he arrested him. This boy doesn't care about anything."

"Well, you're too good for him and that mess. You'll never have a good man in your life if you keep letting that stuff happen," replied Divine.

"I know, Divine. I'll be out of it soon. I miss you," she said, changing the subject.

"That makes two of us, because the feeling is mutual."

"Hey, can you receive picture texts on your phone? I was playing around with my camera phone at the house and took a picture of my sexy piercing I got a few weeks ago. I want to share it with you, if you don't mind."

"That's cool. I don't mind. Send it to me. I'll go ahead and hang up now because I may be heading to bed soon anyway," replied Divine, ending the call.

When Divine's phone alerted him that he had a text message, he opened the message and was surprised to see a picture of Hope's sexy, naked body. Her breasts looked like some Reese cups, with smooth peanut butter skin and chocolate nipples. She was posed in front of a mirror with her legs spread apart. As Divine studied the picture closely, he noticed Hope had her clitoris pierced.

"Damn," he said, while licking his lips.

He then scrolled down and read the message Hope had sent with the picture. *Baby, this is what you've missed over the years. I can't wait until I visit and we make love again. I often dream about it.*"

Divine called Hope back and she answered the phone giggling.

"Girl, what in the hell have you turned into? A freak?" questioned Divine.

"No, boy, I'm just willing to explore and try new things," she replied.

"Damn, things have changed a lot. And something has loss its hair. Is it balding from old age?" laughed Divine.

"Shut up! That makes it better for you to slide your tongue across," jabbed Hope.

"Don't tease me, because I have a craving," responded Divine.

"Don't worry, when I cum all on your face, you'll need some napkins. My oh my! I'll be getting my plane ticket to visit soon for the weekend of the Super Bowl, so tell all your little friends that the wife is coming into town. Damn, I want to sex you so bad."

Just then, the reality of his situation hit him in the face like a semi-truck. He thought about the possibility of Hope and Destiny bumping heads. He hesitated for a few seconds before responding.

"Hope, I respect your body and the knucklehead you can't rid of. I'm not going to lie and say I don't adore you, but I'm not going to lie about something simple either. Honestly, I get confused with you and don't know how to take you at times. Let's just start anew by being friends first."

"Please tell me you're not seeing anyone," Hope said, praying Divine had not moved on.

Although, Divine wanted to deny it, he knew this was his true test to tell the girl he cared about that he had feelings for another woman.

"Yeah, I am seeing someone now," responded Divine after taking a deep breath.

"You're kidding me, right?" replied Hope, feeling as though her heart had just taken a dive off the top of the Empire State Building with no parachute.

"No, I'm not kidding," Divine said in a shallow voice. *Dang, I can't believe I'm doing this,* he thought.

"Who is she?"

"Her name is Destiny. We met at church and just hit it off."

"I feel so embarrassed," Hope said, as she began to cry. "If I knew you were seeing someone, I wouldn't have sent that and been disrespectful," said Hope apologetically.

"Sweetie, you're okay. Stop crying. It's my fault for not saying anything earlier and making little flirtatious comments for it to get to this point. Don't worry about it; we're cool. We're friends. Now go ahead and get some rest. I'll talk to you later."

"Well, I'm glad we're still friends. I want you to be happy. Just don't diss me and make me feel unwanted as a friend," smiled Hope through her tears, as Divine assured her that he wouldn't before they ended their conversation.

CHAPTER 15

A few months passed with Divine working for his uncle Earl cleaning huge buildings at night and sometimes during the day. One night, while at work with his uncle, Divine asked him how he got into the cleaning business.

"Well, when I retired from the army, I worked part-time at a school as a janitor for years before a new principal and staff, who possessed poor management skills, came in and started mistreating the custodians. Therefore, unhappy with my current working conditions, I decided to do something about it. So, I saved part of my retirement check and all of my school board checks in order to gain the capital needed to start my own cleaning business. After several months of networking, I landed a few contracted jobs and managed to launch my business," explained Uncle Earl.

"Wow, it must be nice having your own business and being your own boss," Divine replied.

"Yes, but it also involves having a lot of discipline and responsibility. I had to start off with hands-on work and on-site management until I was able to get my business off the ground. But, son, always remember that you can always build an empire if your heart is in it," the wise man told him.

While in the middle of cleaning floors and talking, Divine's phone rang; it was Destiny.

"Hey, sweetums, I know you're hard at work, but I just wanted you to know that you were on my mind and that I'm so thankful that God blessed me with you in my life. I do hope that our day of committing to be together forever comes soon," Destiny said, shooting a clue as to her interest in becoming his wife.

"I'm sure it will, and it may be sooner than you think," replied

Divine, catching on quickly to her hint.

"Okay, well, get back to work. I miss you already. Love you."

"I miss and love you, too. Sweet dreams, baby," said Divine, then blew her a kiss over the phone before hanging up.

As Divine went back to cleaning the floor, his uncle Earl looked at him with a proud smile.

"So, what young lady has you smiling like that and saying you love her?" asked Uncle Earl, as Divine chuckled.

"Her name is Destiny, and you know what? I think she may be the girl for me to start a family with," said Divine, as his uncle began to cough heavily. "Are you okay, Unc?"

"Yeah, I'm fine. Just a little dust getting in the old lungs, I guess," he replied, gaining control. "Well, I see you guys have the communication part down if she's calling you and having you smile like that at one o'clock in the morning. You do know that lack of communication is one of the key issues that cause marriages to fail, right?"

"Yeah, I know. We actually communicate very well. I'm just afraid it's too soon to marry a girl that I just met a few months ago," stated Divine out of nervousness.

"Well, Divine, no one really has time to waste. If you trust and believe by good judgment of your own merits that she's the one for you, then as a grown man, you should provide for and plan with your future wife. If you guys set goals and continue to work at them, you guys won't end up having a flawed mission. Son, don't be afraid. If you have a great opportunity, pray on it and seize the moment. Now my question to you is do you think you're ready?" asked Uncle Earl.

"Yes, I'm ready," replied Divine with a joyful heart.

"Well, show her that you're ready with a small token." Uncle Earl winked, and then looked down to the ring finger on his left hand to make it clear as to what he was talking about.

"Thanks, Uncle Earl, for the man-to-man talk. I'm going to make you happy," Divine said, hugging his uncle.

"No, put God first, Destiny as your wife second, and your family third, with everyone else finding a spot to get in where they fit in," replied Uncle Earl. "And make sure you stay in your bible and seek God's word first before you react to anything," he added before they started back working.

The next morning, before going their separate ways, Uncle Earl talked to Divine at his car for a minute. "Divine, I was serious when talking to you earlier. If you feel strongly about this girl, make sure you get her something nice to show it. Since you're getting a decent Christmas bonus, you can use that as your way of showing your appreciation for what she means to you in your life."

"Okay," smiled Divine, while pulling off in his car and thinking, *Dang, Uncle Earl is taking this to a whole 'nother level. One would think he is the one considering getting engaged.*

CHAPTER 16

Divine and Destiny's involvement with one another became deeper as time passed. When Divine woke up around 11 a.m. after having worked the nightshift, he often went to Destiny's job to take her out to lunch. Once, when she emerged from the building, he surprised her with two single roses he had purchased from the corner convenience store. During their lunch dates, they ate, laughed, and talked, enjoying the company of one another. With the two growing closer and finally labeling their relationship as 'dating', they spent most of their free time together. With the words '*I love you*' ending phone conversations and being left on voicemails throughout the day, Destiny and Divine found themselves at the point where they were ready to focus on marriage and building a family within the next year.

In the meantime, Faith had officially moved to Atlanta and secured a job at the same mortgage company that Destiny worked at. The two became very close associates, although they didn't know just yet the bond they shared, which was Divine.

Let me fill out a credit application for a jewelry account, Divine thought as he entered the jewelry store, hoping to springboard his and Destiny's relationship towards marriage.

Upon approval, Divine looked over the engagement rings in the glass display case before choosing a 5-karat platinum ring for his future wife.

"Wow, you must really love this lady to get her such a nice ring," the saleswoman commented, while calculating the cost once the in-store discount was applied that they issued to new customers who opened a credit account.

"Yeah, I do. I just want her to be taken care of and comfortable," replied Divine with deep devotion.

"You know, you don't find too many guys like that these days. Shoot, I wish I had a guy doing this for me. This is so sweet."

"It will happen for you. But, look, I'm going to bring my lady by here a little later after she gets off work. I'm going to act like we are just coming to look at a few rings. When in all actuality, I've already purchased the ring I will present to her when I propose. I will need your assistance, though, in persuading her to select the ring I've chosen. Okay?"

"Bring her on by. I got ya," replied the saleswoman, then handed Divine her business card before he left out the door.

That evening, Divine called Destiny and told her to meet him at the jewelry store so they could look at a few rings to see what taste she had. After Destiny got off work, she met Divine at the crowded jewelry store, along with the other customers who were trying to wrap up their Christmas shopping.

Following the plan she had already concocted, the saleswoman pulled four different styles of rings from the case and placed them on the counter in front of Destiny.

"Wow, all of these look very nice, but they're too pricey. I'd rather select a cheaper ring," Destiny said after looking at the beautiful, sparkling rings.

"Well, we have some beauties that are on sale, and Divine has already opened up an account with us. We'll just have to find a style that fits your budget," said the accommodating saleswoman.

"Destiny, take your time to look. I have to run to the car to get my card," Divine said before exiting the store.

"Girl, you have a good man," the saleswoman commented.

"Thank you. I do realize I'm blessed," Destiny replied humbly.

"Well, these are some of our newest, most classy, and elegant rings. And this one here is the crown with honors of the store," added the woman, as she picked up the ring Divine had already purchased. "This is a very rare cut that's stunning and stylish. The diamonds sit perfect and catch the eye of anyone with just a simple movement. Here, try it on."

"Actually, this is the one I like the best, but I know it's in another ballpark in price. This is a gorgeous ring, though," responded Destiny, while moving her hand around a little to see it sparkle in the light. "Out of curiosity, how much does something like this cost?" When the saleswoman showed her the price tag, Destiny replied, "Are you crazy? We could never afford anything like this."

As Divine walked back in, Destiny quickly covered the ring on her finger with her right hand.

"Woo, it's cold out there," Divine said upon entering the store with a coat draped over one arm. "So how's the ring selection coming along?"

"It's going great actually. I think she has chosen a beautiful ring that she's fallen in love with," exclaimed the saleswoman.

"Oh yeah?" replied Divine, as he gently wrapped her in the tanned animal-skin coat. "Well, let me see the ring you have chosen," whispered Divine in Destiny's ear.

"Divine, what are you doing? And whose beautiful coat is this?" questioned Destiny, while turning around to face him.

"It's yours. Now let me see the rock you've chosen because I indeed need a solid rock to stand beside me," Divine replied, giving Destiny a look of admiration.

"This is the ring," Destiny responded, showing him the ring.

"Alright, we'll take it," he told the saleswoman, as Destiny removed the ring from her finger, handed it back to the saleswoman, and began to cry. "What's wrong?" he asked, comforting his lady.

"I just didn't know if anyone would ever care about me so much that they would do the things you do for me," said Destiny.

"It's not always me. I'm just doing what I'm here on earth to do, and that's to love you," replied Divine, and then he leaned over to give her a peck on the lips. "Destiny," he continued, while taking both of her hands in his and looking deeply into her eyes, "rarely does one get a choice at a great deal when you have quantity in your life. That's why I'm choosing the quality in my Destiny." He paused as he dropped down on one knee. "Destiny, will you marry me?" asked Divine with a tear in his eye, while pulling out the ring he had purchased earlier that day from his coat pocket.

Everyone in the store grew quiet as they waited on Destiny's response to his proposal.

"Yes, I'll marry you," responded Destiny.

As soon as she spoke the words, the room exploded with cheering and clapping as Divine stood up to hug and kiss his future wife.

When Divine slid the ring on her finger, they found it was the perfect fit and needed no sizing. The customers continued clapping and congratulating them, even giving them pats on their backs and high-fives, as they exited the store.

"Come on, baby. Let's head back to the house," said Divine, as he opened the door for her.

"Wow, you're so kind. Thank you for opening the door for me," Destiny replied while smiling.

"Don't thank me. Chivalry isn't dead," joked Divine, as he proceeded to clear a path on the pavement with his foot so Destiny wouldn't slip on the snow on her way out.

"Hey, girl, what are you doing up here?" asked a woman who was walking towards the jewelry store's entrance.

"Child, I'm up here with my fiancé. I'm engaged now," Destiny said, while extending her left hand to show off her ring. "He just proposed to me in front of everyone in the jewelry store. It took my breath away."

When Divine let go of the door and turned around to see who Destiny was bragging to, he almost had a heart attack.

"Divine, honey, this is my co-worker Faith."

Oh fuck! thought Divine. His heart dropped and his stomach turned as he starred at Faith, whose eyes were hidden behind her black sunglasses with a diamond logo on the sides.

"Fiancé? Divine is your fiancé?" inquired Faith in surprise, while Destiny quickly confirmed her announcement. "Wow, Divine," Faith mumbled in a low tone. Although she was smiling on the outside, she felt her heart breaking into pieces on the inside.

"Hello, Faith. It's nice to see you again," said Divine, while trembling in fear, not knowing what would come out of Faith's mouth. The ghost from his past had appeared from out of nowhere and with no warning.

"You two know each other?" Destiny quickly interrupted, as she swiftly looked back and forth at the two to find out how they could know each other when Faith was new to the city.

"Yes, Destiny, we know each other well," replied Faith while looking at Divine, whose expression was that of a deer who was caught in headlights.

"Yes, baby, we know each other through conversations. Faith is a woman that Cherish and I met on a cruise. It was nice seeing you again, Faith, but we must hurry and go pick up my daughter Desire.

Enjoy your holiday," rushed Divine, as he grabbed Destiny's hand and pulled her off quickly.

He has no consideration for my feelings, and he doesn't care. He just acts like I was just something to do. I fell for love at first sight, and he used it to his advantage to get what he wanted. All I wanted is for him to love me the way I love him. Yet, he goes and puts a ring on her finger, thought the short-tempered Faith, as she looked from inside of the jewelry store through the falling snow at Divine walking Destiny to her car and giving her a kiss before he closed the door.

CHAPTER 17

After Destiny picked up Desire from daycare, she met Divine at his apartment, where they began to open up a little about each other and come to an agreement on a wedding day. Just as the two were getting ready to talk, Hope called Divine.

"Hello! Hope, I'll give you a call back in a few," said Divine as he hung up the phone.

"Who was that?" asked Destiny.

"Oh, that was just a friend of mine named Hope. She's friends with Danny Boy and all of us," replied Divine.

"See, Divine, this is what I'm talking about," she responded in a blunt voice, as Divine gave her a puzzled look. "You claim you love me and want to marry me, but that's such a lie. I don't like to be lied to. I've told you about these women calling you, and I don't like the fact that you're still allowing it to happen."

"I'm a firm believer in you reap what you sow, and I'm not trying to lead you on. Hope is a friend from high school who is not a threat to you. She's a great woman like you, and has been in a 5-year relationship with her boyfriend. Look, Hope..." explained Divine, accidentally calling Destiny by Hope's name.

"What did you just say?" Destiny asked, cutting off Divine, while rising up from off the couch, rolling her eyes, and looking like she wanted to smack the taste out of his mouth.

Damn, I done fucked up, Divine thought. "Look, Destiny..."

"Oh hell no! I know you didn't just call me her name."

"I was getting ready to say is that Hope is a longtime friend and I don't have to hide anything from you. I want to go into this marriage with honesty and being upfront. I don't want us to be disloyal to our friends just because we get married. Would you rather I get up and go in the bathroom or outside to use the phone?" asked Divine. "If I did that, you'd still get upset with me, thinking I'm hiding something."

"You're right. Forget it, Divine. I don't like the idea of having to beg someone to stop talking to other females when they're in a relationship with me," replied Destiny, while taking off the engagement ring.

"Oh my God! You're kidding, right?" Divine said, refusing to take the ring that Destiny had outstretched toward him.

"No, Divine I'm not kidding or putting on a show for you. I see that it doesn't matter to you how I feel. I don't understand how you could compare me to another woman unless you're spending time with her or you've been talking to her lately. So, I wish you nothing but the best," she said before grabbing her keys and heading to the front door.

"Wait!" Divine shouted, jumping up off the couch and pulling her by her right arm.

"What? What do we have to talk about? You've said what you needed to say. In fact, you said a little too much when you called me by another woman's name. I asked you to do a simple thing and it just hurts my feelings that you won't do it. I just knew you would do that for me just because of the fact that I asked you to. I don't even know what to think of you right now. You shouldn't say things that you don't mean. I knew you were what I thought you were. Playa, please don't call me. You're good. Call Hope. Do what you do. I have no more time to waste on you. I have to go serve the Lord," Destiny concluded, as she left to head for the evening church service.

After sitting on the couching beating himself up about what was right and wrong about having friends while in a relationship, Divine couldn't figure out how a great day could instantly turn into a hell day. With all that was running through Divine's head, he decided he needed a word from the Lord, as well. So, he left out the door not long behind Destiny.

While the choir had its normal prayer before service in the side meeting room, Divine went up to Director Dawn and said, "Take a look at Destiny's finger at her new present."

"Are you serious, Divine?" replied the excited director in disbelief.

"Yep, take a look at what God has done," smiled Divine, knowing God was working miracles in his relationship department.

"Okay," Director Dawn replied while snickering. While she waited with Divine as Destiny walked up with her friends, she told everyone else to head inside the church.

"Congratulations, Divine," said one of Destiny's friends.

"So what's the congratulations for?" poked Director Dawn.

"Look," replied Destiny, while holding up her left hand to show off her ring.

"Oh girl, it's gorgeous," said Director Dawn, as she looked at Divine, who stood with his hands behind his back.

"I must say, Director, the lady has some good taste," Divine commented, trying to get back in Destiny's good graces.

"Whatever, Divine. We're going to stay engaged, but it won't go any further unless you get rid of your closet skeletons, which is Hope," replied Destiny, putting Divine's business all out there while Director Dawn looked on at the two of them.

Intervening, Director Dawn said, "I need to see you both after church. Right now, let's go praise God."

After service, Director Dawn met with Destiny, while Divine went to get Desire from daycare. After picking up Desire and returning to the congregation to play with Desire, Divine waited patiently while Destiny spoke with Director Dawn about him and her issues with his friends.

"Look," said Director Dawn, "I'm going to speak with Divine for a few minutes, but I'm going to need you guys to set up marriage counseling before you get married." Destiny agreed to her suggestion. "Divine, come here for a second," shouted Director Dawn, as she called him over to speak with him for a bit before telling him about the counseling and how it would help their marriage.

With the two agreeing to meet with the pastor for marriage counseling, Director Dawn set up an appointment for the following Tuesday.

Right before walking into their first counseling session, Divine turned to Destiny and said, "Let's be upfront and honest with Pastor. I'm going to still love you the same, so let's just tell Pastor the truth and not be secretive or withhold anything. Okay?"

Destiny agreed to his request, and they entered the church.

Before the pastor started with questions regarding marriage, he stressed the importance of being honest so they could get to the root of any present problems that may violate the sanctity of their marriage if not addressed before the exchange of vows.

As the pastor proceeded with the questions, the two got a feel for what exactly they were getting into. The pastor asked Destiny first about what she liked in Divine, and she pointed out all the good qualities of Divine, which included him spoiling her. When asked what she disliked about Divine, she expressed she felt uncomfortable with the close relationship he had with his female friends. As Destiny spoke, the pastor jotted down notes. Then, the pastor asked Divine the same questions. Divine replied that he liked Destiny for her humbleness, but that at times, it seemed as if he was dating two people because of the way she reacted to certain things.

Destiny instantly gave Divine a stern look, tilted her head, and folded her arms across her chest. "What do you mean by that?" interrupted Destiny.

"You'll have your chance to talk Destiny in a minute. Go on, Divine," the pastor said, wanting to maintain order during the session and allow them to hear each other out.

"It's nothing major. It just seems like small insecurity and self-esteem issues get in the way of us communicating at times," Divine added.

"Well, you two have to come to an agreement as one and do what is best for the relationship. Divine, as a mate, you have to help boost and build her self-esteem, and Destiny, you have to know that if Divine likes you and shows you that he cares by giving you small gifts, he may be trying to make you feel welcome and comfortable. Both of you have to learn to come together in the time of adversity and not depart," explained the Pastor, while Divine looked over at Destiny, who was agreeing with everything the Pastor was saying.

I love you, Destiny mouthed, as she smiled at Divine, who replied by mouthing, *I love you, too.*

As Destiny and Divine left the counseling session, Divine told Destiny to stop by his apartment so they could talk out some more issues and start planning for their future together.

CHAPTER 18

When Faith arrived at the office the next morning, she went out of her way to stop at the front desk to talk to Destiny. Faith looked her up and down as she helped herself to a peppermint out of the candy bowl Destiny had on her desk, while waiting for her to finish up a call.

"Hey, girl, how are you?" asked Destiny, as she hung up the phone and jotted down something on a notepad.

"I'm doing well. I'm just excited that the season has changed and it has brought snow. Hey, are you going to be around for lunch? I wanted to talk to you about some business," questioned Faith.

"Yeah, my ears are always open to listen to some business opportunities."

"Good, you can ride with me to lunch. Is eleven-thirty okay?" Faith asked.

"That's fine," Destiny replied, as Faith proceeded to her office to get some work done.

When eleven-thirty rolled around, Faith put on her tinted butterscotch Dolce & Gabbana shades and went to the front to pick up Destiny.

"I'm sorry I'm parked so far, but I got here late," said Faith, making conversation as they walked to her car.

"Child, that's not a problem. I need the exercise anyway. I'm looking for an all-women's gym so I can feel comfortable while trying to get in shape. I don't like when guys stare or hound me when I'm working out," replied Destiny.

"Well, for me, I think the co-ed gym is a plus because of some of the sexy brothers that be working out," laughed Faith, as she pushed the alarm on the key fob of her black S550 Mercedes that sat high on rims.

"Dang, Faith, I need to be making some of that money your making," said Destiny in awe, as she got inside the car. "Ooo, girl, I like this leather interior."

"Well, thank you. You can have my car note and insurance payments if you want them," Faith chuckled, while pulling off toward the restaurant.

As they sat having lunch, Faith took this opportunity to get to befriend her opponent. You know what they say, "Keep your friends close and your enemies closer."

"Well, Destiny, I'm new to the Atlanta area and came here for many different reasons, which include change and better opportunities. So, tell me what exactly it is that you do up front as a secretary."

"I take calls and file paperwork."

"So would you be interested in becoming my real estate assistant?" inquired Faith.

"What do I have to do?" Destiny asked, while thinking about the way Faith was always dressed in suits, carrying expensive designer bags, and driving around in the latest series model Mercedes. "I know I'm too advanced for my position, and I am looking for something new anyway. I like to be challenged, and would love to move up in the firm," replied Destiny with interest.

"You have to get your sales license to work for me," Faith informed her as the waiter placed their food on the table. "Destiny, I'm a real estate agent now and am licensed in several states, but I'm trying to start my new development for low-income housing with parks here in the area. You mentioned before that you wanted to move up in the mortgage firm, but I need a licensed assistant as part of my team," stated Faith.

"Well, I'll start working on my license soon," Destiny replied.

"Please do, because I think you'll suit the position well. It will also give you a lot of experience in the real estate industry, which is very competitive."

During the course of the lunch, Faith created a relaxed atmosphere between her and Destiny, hoping that Destiny would feel comfortable enough with her to keep her in the loop of the happenings of her professional and personal life, and it worked. By the time lunch was over, Destiny felt a bond between her and Faith;

however, it was unbeknown to her what Faith's true intentions really were as a result of this newfound friendship.

"Hey, girl, how are things going with you? I haven't seen you in a few days," said Faith, stopping by Destiny's desk after arriving at work.

"Things are going pretty well," replied Destiny, as she took hold of the stack of papers she was about to punch holes in. When she did this, the glimmer of her ring caught Faith's eye and sparked some jealousy.

As Destiny continued to talk to Faith, thinking she was getting closer to her future business partner, Faith stood in disgust, internally fuming over Destiny and Divine's recent engagement. As she half-listened to Destiny go on and on about the wedding plans she would need to make in the upcoming months, she plotted her next move.

"That's good to hear, Destiny. Well, let me know if you need anything, and don't forget to start handling your business in regards to the credentials for the real estate assistant position," said Faith, before going into her office and closing the door to isolate herself.

I can't believe this. It's a shame that I got to go through all this to prove my love to someone. Let me call his ass to see what's up with this bullshit, thought Faith as she dialed Divine's number. "Good morning, Divine. I didn't mean to wake you, but I was wondering if you wanted to join me at a concert this weekend. I won backstage passes from the morning show call in, and wanted to invite you to come along with me."

"I'm sorry, but I won't be able to go on a one-on-one date with you, Faith. You're my friend and Destiny knows of you, but I'm going to have to talk it over with my fiancée," replied Divine, while thinking back to what Destiny had said about disliking his friends during their marriage counseling session.

"That's fucked up. It hurts so much to hear you say that, and your engagement has hurt me more than you could ever realize. I moved down here to be closer to you so we could work on us," said Faith, expressing her outrage.

"I didn't tell you to do that," responded Divine with a nonchalant attitude.

"You know what, Divine? I understand and have no ill feelings. I'll be alright because you don't deserve the luxury of being with me anyway," remarked Faith.

"Whatever, Faith. God bless you," Divine said, ending their conversation.

"Dang, Divine, how you just going to blow me off like that for a few days?" laughed Hope, when Divine finally got around to returning her call.

"I'm sorry. We need to talk, Hope," Divine said in a solemn tone.

"What do we need to talk about, Mr. Divine?"

"Well, I called to inform you that you were one of the topics in me and Destiny's marriage counseling the other day," Divine divulged.

"Excuse me? Marriage what?" replied Hope, before dropping the phone as her heart skipped a few beats. "Please tell me that you're kidding about your little comment," she said upon picking the phone back up and placing it to her ear.

"No, Hope, I'm being honest," replied Divine.

"Boy, you know I'm a huge bag of emotions right now, filled with hurt, sadness, and fear of you rushing into something." A few tears of joy fell from her eyes as she spoke. "But you know what, Divine? Through all these mixed emotions, I'm not one bit angry. If you feel like she's the woman for you, I'm happy for you. Just invite me to the wedding and know that it's a missed opportunity for you with me," stated Hope graciously.

"Hell, it's one for you, too, Ms. 'I'ma help him until he gets on his feet'," teased Divine as he laughed.

"Shut up, married man. His sorry ass is supposed to be outta here when he gets his income tax check in January. I don't see how without a job, but we'll see," replied Hope.

"Well, I'm not hitched yet," hinted Divine.

"Oh Lord, I take this as one of those calls where you have to cut me off as a friend. Correct?"

"Dang, you sure can read between the lines," responded Divine.

"I know a little something. Most insecure mates that have a tendency to cheat always want you to cut off the friends, especially the ones you've been sexual with or they feel threatened by," replied Hope.

"It's the hardest thing for me to do with you, though. Hope, we have so much more than a marriage or mate can break up," Divine

Deaubrey Devine

expressed.

"I know, Divine, but that's all a part of being married. If you vow that you're ready to be as one, you have to be honest and have trust to lead the way in your marriage. I'm here always for you. We're cool. Just be my friend, and lend a listening ear for me to cry in at times. Cherish your wife. Don't push her away for a friendship," added Hope, giving her blessings for Divine's marriage.

"Thanks, friend," Divine responded in a content voice.

"Okay, buddy. Now let me get off this phone before I get to preaching up in here," laughed Hope after giving Divine advice concerning his new relationship adventure.

Before getting married, Divine and Destiny thought it would be a good idea for them to all stay in Divine's apartment for a week to see if they could live together as a family. During this time, the two shared the different highs and lows of their life.

One night, Divine told his family to get on their knees so they could start a tradition of praying together as a family before they went to sleep. Destiny thought Divine's prayer was a bit long, as he prayed a hedge of protection over nearly every area of their lives in detail for almost five minutes.

"D, I appreciate you stepping up to take control and be the head to lead us in prayer," said Destiny.

"We have to start things off right," Divine replied, as they all climbed into bed, where he held Destiny while she held Desire.

The next morning, Destiny got up to cook breakfast for the family. Not long after Destiny left to go in the kitchen, Desire rolled over toward Divine. He put his arms around her to give her a hug, and when he did, he found out that she had wet the bed. As Divine tried to wake Desire up so he could change her and the sheets, he learned quickly that Desire wasn't a morning person when she began to cry. Destiny, who heard her daughter crying, dropped everything to come in the room to see what was going on.

"Look at her bad dream that scared her," Divine said, while pointing to the wet spot in the bed.

"I'm so sorry," Destiny apologized.

"It's okay. It's our fault for not having her use the bathroom before bed. We just can't give her anything to drink before she goes to bed from now on, baby," replied Divine, as Destiny smiled at his

114

understanding. "I got little momma. Come on, big girl. Let's get up and take a bath," said Divine, as he walked Desire into the bathroom so he could run her a bath and play in the bubbles with her as he bathed her.

After drying her off, he held her up to the sink and taught her how to brush her teeth to the Ole McDonald farm tune, as she got into the song and said, "A quack quack here and a quack quack there," while laughing the whole time.

"Go, girl," Divine said, encouraging Desire to brush every little spot as Destiny stood in the doorway and smiled.

"Divine, you're something else. I've had to fight to get her up and ready every morning, and you worked some magic to get her to cooperate on your first try. You know I'm jealous," said Destiny, as Divine smiled at Desire.

"Mummy, teeth," said Desire in a slurred speech, while cheesing to show off her cleaned teeth.

"I'm just trying to build an infrastructure bridge," Divine replied.

"Yes, so I see. This proves to me even more that you're the perfect father for my daughter," replied Destiny.

Divine went to the door and gave his treasure a hug.

"Okay, let's hurry up and eat so I can drop Desire off at daycare," said Destiny.

"Don't try to rush. Take your time. I can drop her off," Divine offered.

"Awww, thanks. That will be a big help. I'll call and tell them to add your name to the pick-up and drop-off list. She's been meeting with a speech pathologist three times a week, so you may have to get a schedule of the times she meets when you drop her off. Wow, Divine, you're making life so much easier for me by sharing my world," stated Destiny.

"That's why I was created. Babe, does she need lunch money?" asked Divine.

"Boy, no! You're acting like she's in high school," laughed Destiny.

"I'm just checking," Divine replied with a chuckle. "You know this is all new to me."

"You're funny. Let me hurry because I'm running a little late," Destiny said, then rushed off to finish getting dressed.

While she was getting dressed, Cherish called Divine and told him that the cleaning company was having the Christmas party the next day.

"Dang, this is a short notice, but I'll make sure I'm there" said Divine.

"Well, check your email more often. Anyway, thanks for telling me about your engagement to my girl," replied Cherish sarcastically since she found out from a church member instead of her cousin.

"My bad, cuz," giggled Divine.

"That's okay. Divine, I see how you leave your favorite cuz in the dark," responded Cherish, as Divine howled on the phone.

"Girl, you know I love you," said Divine, just as Destiny walked past with a curious look.

"Divine, who are you telling that you love them?" questioned Destiny.

"This is Cherish. She called to tell us about the Christmas party tomorrow."

"Oh, tell her that I said hello," Destiny replied.

"Tell her I said hello, also. Well, congratulations, and make sure you bring your fiancée because everyone wants to meet her," Cherish said before hanging up.

"You and Cherish are really close, huh?" Destiny asked after she finished getting dressed.

"Yeah, that's my boo," replied Divine, as he smiled and told Destiny that his family wanted to meet her.

"I want to meet them, too," Destiny said, as she ran to give Desire a kiss and then went to give Divine a hug and kiss before dashing out the door for work.

Instead of dropping Desire off at the daycare center, Divine decided he would take the opportunity to build a bond with his future stepdaughter. He concentrated on helping Desire with sounding out simple words in an attempt to help her with her speech. They also shared quality time of reading, writing, and spending a day at the park. While riding in the car, Divine played his breakthrough song "Say the Name". He heard Desire humming the word *Jesus* that was said repeatedly in the song, but when he looked in the rearview mirror at her, Desire quickly grew silent and cracked a smile.

"Sing it, Desire," Divine said, but she only looked at him and continued to smile as he started the song over from the beginning. When Desire and Divine arrived back home, they met Destiny who had dinner on the stove cooking. Divine took a seat in the living room with Desire, and the two watched a cartoon movie while waiting for dinner to be ready. While eating, Divine and Destiny decided to get married in March, which was three months away. After dinner, Destiny left the room to give Desire a bath. When she returned to the kitchen, she found Divine standing at the sink washing the dishes.

"What are you doing?" asked Destiny in shock, while looking at him organizing the pots and plates in the dish rack.

"Washing dishes. It's only right if you cook that I share the responsibility and wash the dishes. Heck, you already have multiple duties as a wife as it is. I only have a few dishes left, and then I can rub your feet for a few minutes," winked Divine.

"Okay," replied Destiny with a gratified expression.

After Divine finished the dishes and put them away, he went and got the lotion to massage Destiny's feet as they talked and laughed, with Desire sitting nearby watching television. With Divine having to go to work that night, he called his uncle to inform him that he'd be a few minutes late and that he would meet him at the site.

Before they all went to lie in bed for a few minutes before he left for work, he took Desire to the bathroom to avoid her mother having to deal with any "accidents" in the middle of the night. When they returned to the bedroom, Desire crawled in the middle of the bed and started humming the song Divine had been playing in his car earlier when they were out.

"Baby, what are you humming?" asked Destiny, as Desire looked at Divine.

"She's singing a simple song that brought me through the storm," Divine replied for Desire, who had started singing the song.

"This is very surprising. Did you teach her that?" asked Destiny, while smiling.

"No, she just picked it up while riding in the car," replied Divine, as he joined Desire in singing.

Not much later, Desire had fallen asleep. Divine leaned over and gave Desire a kiss upon her forehead and his future wife a kiss upon her lips, before pulling the covers over them and leaving for work.

CHAPTER 19

Divine, I moved to Atlanta to be closer to you. That may sound crazy since I didn't discuss it with you first, but I thought that was what you wanted. You gave me false hope and sent me mixed messages when you slept with me. I was very hurt to find out about you getting married. I love you and can't take that kind of hurt anymore, texted Faith in multiple messages when Divine returned home after working an overnight shift with his uncle.

I'm sorry about your hurt, Divine replied, *and I hope things get better for you. But it's reality. I'm marrying Destiny in March.*

Refusing to let that be the end of things, Faith proceeded with her next plan of action. Right before Destiny left for her lunch break, Faith approached her desk.

"So what's my future real estate assistant doing for lunch?" asked Faith.

"Girl, I have to go to the mall to get an outfit with the money Divine gave me so I can meet his family tonight," boasted Destiny.

"Oh, well, do you mind if I ride with you?" asked Faith.

"Shoot, I don't care. Come on, girl. I would enjoy the company," said Destiny, as they left the building and walked to Destiny's car. "You have to excuse my car. Child, you wouldn't know how it is having a four-year-old in your car," Destiny said, while throwing the trash from the front seat onto the backseat to make room for Faith.

"It's okay. I babysit my friend's kids every now and then. So, I know the damage they can do," replied Faith, while thinking to herself, *It's a damn shame for a bitch to be this nasty. I can't believe Divine wants to marry this old quirky-ass dingbat.*

While Destiny was pouncing around shopping and trying on outfits, Faith became jealous at the fact that Destiny would be meeting Divine's family.

"Destiny, I like you a lot…like a sister I never had…and it hurts me to see you walk into something without knowing all the details. I've been beating myself up with whether I should tell you or not, but since there is a child involved, I feel you should know," said Faith, as Destiny stopped to look at her.

"Girl, what's up? What's wrong?" asked Destiny out of great concern.

"It's Divine and Cuz," Faith replied, stressing the word 'cuz'.

"What do you mean by that?" questioned Destiny.

"Well, don't kill the messenger, but I'm just being real. You have no idea about Divine and Cherish. Divine needs to quit fucking with your head and tell you the truth about Cherish before the two of you get married. He's not ready."

"What are you talking about?" Destiny asked, still in a state of confusion.

"Come on, Destiny. Put two and two together. Why in the hell would you go to the Bahamas with your damn cousin and stay in a room with one bed for a few days? The cuz is just a label to throw everyone off. Cherish pretends to be Divine's cousin, but I was with them in the Bahamas, and trust me, what goes on in the Bahamas, stays in the Bahamas. Believe me, honey, it's a lot more than you know. But hey, maybe he's changing for you. If your heart is there, go for it," poured on Faith, playing out her wicked act.

"Well, yesterday morning I did overhear him saying that he loved her," replied Destiny, as she thought back to the conversation.

"See, that's the shit I'm talking about, Destiny. Niggas ain't shit! If that was me, I'd put his dick on a table and hit it with a damn hammer," said the irate Faith, as she played off the words of Destiny, who was now teary eyed.

"Faith, I thought I had found a man that would treat me and my child right. Now I feel like the victim of a hit and run, with many bumps and bruises," exhaled Destiny after taking a deep breath.

Her heartache could not be soothed, but Faith attempted to offer some comfort by hugging her.

"Don't worry about it. Just pray about it. And whatever you do, please don't tell Divine I told you because it will cause so much confusion. Besides that, you'll mess up your inside connection if you do decide to pursue the marriage," emphasized Faith.

"Okay," Destiny simply replied, while still struggling with thoughts of being betrayed by the one person she loved the most besides her daughter.

"Girl, still get that outfit if he's spending like that. Just get what you can out of him like he's getting what he can out of you," said Faith, persuading Destiny to take advantage of Divine's kindness.

"Baby, what's wrong?" asked Divine, as Destiny entered the apartment after returning from work. When she walked through the door, she totally disregarded Divine and went straight to hug Desire after he tried to greet her.

"Nothing's wrong. What time is this party?" asked Destiny curtly.

"Seven o'clock," he replied, wondering if her bad attitude was the result of maybe having a bad day at work.

"Okay, let me take a shower and try to do something to my hair," Destiny replied.

"While you're doing that I'll get myself and Desire dressed," replied Divine.

Minutes later, Destiny entered the living room. "Divine, how does my hair look?"

"It's fine, baby. Come on, you look nice," he said, while placing his arm around her neck to hug her. In the process, his forearm accidentally brushed up against her hair.

"Dang, Divine, you messed my hair up!" yelled Destiny, pushing him off of her.

"I barely touched it. I'm sorry," Divine apologized, as Destiny rushed off to the bathroom and then returned a few minutes later.

"I'm not going!" yelled Destiny.

"What?" shouted Divine, blown away by Destiny's announcement.

"It took me a minute to do something with my hair and then you go and mess it up."

"Well, go bump and curl it, and let's ride," Divine said, wondering what the reason was for Destiny's irritability. "They usually have a surprise for Uncle Earl and his wife at the beginning of the party every year, and I would like to be on time."

"Well, have fun. I can't go anywhere looking like this, and especially if going to meet your family for the first time," stated Destiny.

"Destiny, you mean to tell me you're going to get fully dressed and then say you don't want to go five minutes before it's time for us to leave because of your hair?"

"Yes! And besides, I don't have a babysitter," replied Destiny.

"You don't have to have a babysitter. It's a family affair."

"Well, I'm not going," responded Destiny with an unwilling tone.

"Well, can Desire still go with me?" Divine asked.

"I don't know."

"You know what? You're starting to turn into a real drama queen," Divine said, while taking Desire by the hand.

"Don't you dare stand there and ridicule me. I said I'm not going," replied Destiny with a firm voice.

"Well, the ball is in your court about your decision, but Desire's going."

"Well, drop Desire off at my aunt's house. I'm moving back home," she replied with much attitude, trying to get Divine upset.

"Go ahead, Destiny. I don't know what's up with you and these mood changes," said Divine before he left with Desire for the Christmas party.

As a result of Destiny being insubordinate, Divine arrived at the party late and ended up missing the presentation of Uncle Earl and his wife's surprise. Everyone was excited to meet Desire, but questioned Divine as to why his fiancée was not there with him. He quickly thought of a lie, telling everyone she sick. Once Desire was comfortable with playing with the other children there, Uncle Earl pulled Divine to the side to chat with him.

"She's started already, huh?" Uncle Earl said.

"Yeah, I don't know what's up with her," replied Divine.

"Well, son, just make sure you take your time to think things through with the engagement. Keep going to counseling, and make sure y'all are equally yoked," he said, while handing Divine his bonus check.

"Okay, thanks, Unc," replied Divine with a smile, then returned to mingle with his family.

As he was walking around with Desire and talking to everyone, Cherish asked, "Divine, why are you babysitting and my girl's not here?"

"Destiny's tripping for no reason."

Deaubrey Devine

"Man, let me call her," said Cherish, while dialing Destiny's number. However, when she answered, Destiny told her to never call her or say anything to her again before hanging up on her. "What did you do to her? What's wrong with her?" asked Cherish in a state of bafflement.

"I didn't do anything. I don't know what's up with her. She just came home from work tripping," replied Divine innocently.

"Ooh, unh unh. If I knew Destiny was going to act like this, I wouldn't have introduced y'all to each other."

"Cuz, it's cool. Just pray for us," replied Divine.

After spending several hours with his family, he decided it was time to get Desire home and in the bed. Before dropping her off at her aunt's house, though, Divine drove through the streets of downtown so Desire could see the Christmas lights and the huge decorated tree.

Once he arrived at Destiny's aunt's house, Destiny greeted him at the door.

"Here's a plate, baby," he said, showing his thoughtfulness by bringing her something back to eat. "On the real, this is why I said you be tripping. We're not even married yet and I'm getting stressed out with you."

"Whatever, Divine. You're just too sneaky and conniving for me. I've prayed about you ever since you've been at your little party, but if you care about me and want this marriage to go through, you'd better set up that marriage counseling session tomorrow…quick, fast, and in a hurry. Now, I'm through talking. I'll see you at counseling tomorrow or there will be no wedding. And here's your ring back," she said, as she removed the engagement ring from her finger, handed it to Divine, and then slammed the door in his face, leaving him standing in a state of confusion as to what was going on.

The next afternoon, Divine called his pastor and expressed the need for an emergency appointment for a meeting between him, the pastor, and Destiny. The pastor agreed to meet with the two of them, and said he would count this meeting as the second session of their marriage counseling. After setting the time with the pastor, Divine called Destiny and told her that she needed to meet him at the church when she got off work.

As the heated counseling session began, Divine said, "Pastor, I just want to ask my future wife why she's being so short and rude

122

with me."

"Pastor, with all due respect for your wife, would you call your cousin 'Boo' or tell her you love her?" asked Destiny.

"Well, maybe if the situation permitted, but I don't see anything wrong with expressing love toward a family member," the pastor replied, as Divine looked over at Destiny with a strange expression.

"I know you're not acting like this because of my conversation with Cherish," Divine interrupted.

"You know what, Divine? I am. Also, I need answers on where you and Cherish slept while on your little cruise together, and who else went with the two of on this trip."

After Divine explained the situation, Destiny said, "Exactly my point. He and his so-called cousin have something going on," talking as though she had concrete proof.

"Destiny, that's my cousin!" shouted Divine.

"Yeah, right. And how are you going to have me sit next to your cousin slash creep partner at church after we had sex only days before!" yelled Destiny in anger, as the pastor raised his eyebrows and sat back in his seat to be nosey about the discovery of them engaging in premarital sex.

"Things like this are what have been stressing me lately and it's hectic mentally. I can't understand how my cousin is infringing on our relationship and how you could put our wedding on hold indefinitely because of your accusations of me cheating. Destiny, I love you, and you're truly in my heart. Aside from my God, you, Desire, and my family, nothing else really matters."

After the pastor talked to the two for a few minutes, telling them that God is love and they have to develop a loving relationship, he confronted Divine to ask him were all the allegations against him true.

"No, Cherish is my blood cousin, Pastor, and I don't do family incest," replied Divine.

The pastor then turned his attention to speak to Destiny. "So, Destiny, do you believe him and trust him as your future husband going towards a marriage?"

"I'll think about trying it again if he's honest about Cherish," replied Destiny.

"So where's your heart on willing to try again?" asked the pastor.

"The only way I can see this moving forward is if Divine agrees that we will not have sex before getting married, and focus on making me and Desire the center of his world."

Man, what's up with this dang girl? thought Divine. *How can I focus on her and Desire anymore than I already do. They get every minute of my free time when I'm not at work or serving the Lord.*

"I don't want to shack up, stay the night with you, or have sex before we get married in March. Can you agree to that?" asked Destiny, as Divine looked at the pastor.

"Of course he does, because he knows premarital sex is a sin," said the pastor, answering for Divine.

"Yes, baby, I agree. We can withhold from having sex, and I promise you that I'll still be here because I'm grateful for the blessing that God presented to me in the form of you," he said, as he slipped the ring back on her finger.

CHAPTER 20

With the holiday season now behind them and the time to file income taxes now upon them, Destiny was looking forward to receiving a nice refund from the earned income credit due to her. With that money, she planned to pay off a few bounced checks that resulted from her overspending during Christmas. In addition, she discussed with Divine her plans to pay off some things on her credit report so she could help when it came time for them to invest in a condo or townhome after they were married. However, when Destiny got her income tax check seven days after filing thanks to the rapid anticipation loan, the money didn't stretch as far as she had hoped. She spent all of her refund paying back cash advance loans, Desire's daycare fee that was two months behind, and the fees associated with the bounced checks. In addition, the bank's risk management collections department restricted her from opening another account within a year.

As Destiny tried hard to hide her credit instability from Divine, the stress from her lack of finances put a strain on their relationship. While they had their ups and downs, Divine continued to go into his prayer closet and pray for his family, hoping that everything would work out if he kept the faith. In the meantime, he released himself of his sexual urges by watching his extensive collection of porn movies.

During the second week in January, Divine received a call from Hope while Destiny was at work.

"I apologize for the delay, but Happy New Year."

"Hey, Hope. Happy New Year to you, too. How's everything?" Divine asked.

"Well, since you asked, let me update you on my little soap opera," she said, taking the opportunity to vent to her dear friend.

"When I asked this punk when was he getting his income tax check and getting out because I need to make arrangements, do you know his high-ass grabbed me by both of my arms, pinned me to the wall, and said, 'Look, I'm not going any fucking where now because my check was taken because I owed.' So, that's when I looked him dead in his eyes and told him he needed to go to plan B and get out my place. Well, what did I say that for? This fool tightened his grip on my arms and said, 'We're stuck together like two dogs.' So, I told his ass, 'Well, I'm going to find out if boiling hot water can break two dogs up.' When he let go of me, I told his ass to get the fuck out and then I called the police on his ass. Do you know when the police came they didn't take him because he said that I hit him. Their punk asses said that they would have to take the both of us. It was a total debacle. But by saying all the bad news, the good news on the flip side is I'm still coming in town for Super Bowl weekend to a party, and hopefully when I return to Connecticut, my roommate will be gone," said Hope.

"Yeah, yeah, I'll believe it when I see it. I don't think he's going to be gone when you return, so get ready for the years to come."

"Ha, ha, very funny. Anywho, I really need a ride when I get to the airport in Atlanta. My flight arrives that Friday at seven o'clock in the evening. Of course, I'll have to turn off my phone when the plane takes off, but when it lands, I could be at your family's house a few minutes after you pick me up," said Hope.

"Alright now, don't play like that. I like living," Divine replied.

"I'm just playing. I don't do married men anyway," teased Hope.

"Good, because I don't cheat on people," laughed Divine.

"Thank God for change, because you were off the chain in your younger days."

"You always say that," Divine responded.

"Well, it's true. At least you've grown out of it, though. Some men want to continue playing games even when their grown."

"I know. Well, I'm sorry about the ups and downs you're having with your boyfriend, but I hope things work out for you soon," Divine replied.

Before ending their call, Divine and Hope made a bet with one another about who would win the Super Bowl between the Patriots and the Giants. Divine chose the Patriots, and Hope went with the underdog. Whoever lost the bet promised the other they would send them a gift card to their favorite restaurant.

Since the Patriots ended up losing after a flawless season, Divine found himself having to come out of pocket. However, he didn't mind because when it came down to it, regardless of his feelings for Destiny, he would have given Hope the world.

CHAPTER 21

Not long after completing the last counseling session with success and no negative issues, the big wedding day came. By then, Divine had convinced Destiny that they should have a small wedding with a small reception. His reasoning for this was so they could make sure they were able to start saving their money, build their credit, and move out of Divine's apartment and into a house.

"Wow, Divine, your aunt and Cherish were here early and have everything set up. This wedding ceremony seems like it's going to go really smooth. Are your parents coming?" Director Dawn asked. She knew Destiny's father was nowhere to be found and that her mother had passed away several years ago, but she couldn't remember Divine ever mentioning anything about his parents.

"Unfortunately, they won't be able to attend. I lost them when I was a senior in high school, and have pretty much been by myself since then," replied Divine sorrowfully.

"I'm so sorry to hear that," Director Dawn replied, as the pastor walked in the room.

"My gosh, son, you look sharp as a tack in your tux!" shouted the pastor, as Divine blushed and replied thank you.

"Alright, guys, let me go help seat people coming in," said Director Dawn before she left.

"I glad you and Destiny worked everything out to be ready for this day," the pastor said, while smiling and reaching over to fix Divine's collar.

"Yeah, that's my wife. Pastor, I just want to give that girl all of me and not just a piece of me in our marriage," conveyed Divine.

"Just give your all and keep God first. It'll work if you hear his voice and let him guide you."

"Ok, I take it that I need to be very considerate to my heart then," replied Divine.

"Yes, but also to Destiny's heart because you guys will be one shortly. Do you have the ring?" asked the pastor, as Divine pulled out the ring to show it to him. "Alright, I'll call you in a few," said the pastor as he left Divine sitting on the front row of the church thinking about the life changing step he was about to take.

Meanwhile, as one of Destiny's friends helped her get dressed in the other room, Lemon Head followed Neal into the church.

"Divine, is Precious coming?" asked Neal jokingly, while grabbing Divine to hug him.

"Man, stop playing," Divine replied in a serious tone, as the anger at what Neal had told Precious started to burn inside him again.

"Man, it's been months since we've talked," said the jubilant Neal like nothing never happened.

"Yeah, I know. I've just been with the wife," replied Divine.

"Yeah, I've been in and out of town trying to get serious like you. I've been dating this girl, and thank God for Lemon hooking me up with the discount flights."

"Go for it," Divine replied, glad that his friend was finally settling down. "It's a good thing to be in love. Where's Danny Boy?" asked Divine, while looking around.

"He's outside. His wife is here in the Chapel room with your family and friends," replied Neal.

Outside, Danny Boy was talking to Hope on the phone.

"Chic, where are you? You know Divine is going to freak out when he sees you in the audience. He doesn't know that you have a surprise ticket. I thought you would be here so I could tell him that you're going to stop the wedding and he could be nervous at the altar anticipating you stopping the ceremony," laughed Danny Boy.

"I don't think I'm going to make it because it's going to cost too much for me to get my flight changed. Besides, I wouldn't get there until tonight. I'm so fucking pissed now because I let this asshole hold my car to go see his probation officer and he picked the wrong day to come back two and a half hours late to pick me up. I've missed my flight, and I'm upset to the point that I'm crying. I may go visit my friends who live about two hours and forty-five minutes north of Connecticut just so I can get away from his dumb-ass," Hope said, pissed about her plans being ruined.

"I'm sorry about that happening to you. See, if you and Divine would have gone on and took care of business when y'all hooked back up, he would be marrying you instead of this girl."

"That's your boy running to the altar all fast like he's at a track meet," Hope replied.

"I know. I told him that he's just whipped," said Danny Boy.

"He better not be, because he hasn't hit this in a while. Divine knows that I'm his soul mate," Hope said, feeling as though her heart was breaking into a million pieces.

"Well, look, I'm sorry I have to cut this short, but the ceremony is about to start. I'll tell Divine you send your congratulations and best wishes."

As Destiny walked down the aisle to altar, while waving at a few guests like she was Ms. America, Divine stood in awe at her beauty.

Before the pastor started with the ceremonial speech, Divine mouthed to Destiny how beautiful she looked, while Destiny expressed the same about how handsome he was.

After the pastor pronounced them man and wife, Faith exited the church undetected by Divine or Destiny.

Immediately after the small reception, Divine and Destiny departed in the limo for a tour of the city before arriving at the hotel resort that Uncle Earl and his wife paid for so they could enjoy their first night together as man and wife.

When they arrived in the lobby, the front desk agent couldn't check them in fast enough for Divine. He was all too eager to finally be able to make love to Destiny after their long stint of abstinence. However, once they were inside the room, things didn't work out as Divine had hoped. When he approached Destiny to help her remove her dress, he was quickly rejected with a slight push from her.

"What's the matter?" he asked in a puzzled tone.

"I'm sick and don't feel very well," she replied.

"Sick how?" questioned Divine.

"If you must know, I'm on my period," said Destiny rudely.

Unfazed by her comment, Divine smirked. "Well, it's a good thing we're two adults and can please each other in more than one way."

"Well, let's get this clear. I don't feel like doing anything tonight because I'm sick and having a girly day, so don't be trying to force me to do something that I don't feel like doing. I just want to take some ibuprofen and go to bed," Destiny said miserably.

Divine tried his best not to get upset and did not want to be selfish, but still, he had needs, too. "Destiny, this special friend of yours misses you," hinted Divine.

"And I miss the colossal, too, but it's going to have to wait a few more days to get taken care of," replied Destiny as Divine frowned.

"So you're not going to play with it or nothing?" Divine asked.

"Look, Divine, I told you I don't feel like it, but I'll think about it if you leave me alone. Dang, let me rest for a few minutes and take a shower," replied Destiny, growing irritated with his persistence.

Divine's anger and disappointment caused him to become silent.

"What's wrong?" Destiny asked.

"Nothing," replied Divine curtly.

"So you have an attitude now because I'm on my period?"

"That's not the point. I would do anything you ask of me because I want to please my wife. However, you act like you can't do the same for me," explained Divine, who felt like he was being treated unfair.

"Well, let freedom ring, Divine, with that reverse psychology you just tried to pull. I feel that you're trying to manipulate me and use your little metaphor to benefit you. But like I said, I'll think about it since it's a big deal to you. I'll do it when I'm ready and get at it later if I'm up to it. Right now, though, I'm going to take a shower."

After Destiny disappeared into the bathroom, Divine laid across the bed fuming at the thought of not being able to consummate their marriage that night. *Man, this is some bullshit.*

The next morning as the sun rose, Divine woke up to Destiny giving him some good old-fashion head.

"Damn, baby," whispered Divine, as he palmed the back of her head with both hands and played in her hair. "Girl, where did you learn those skills from?"

"I'm just pleasing my husband like he pleases his wife," responded Destiny as she continued bobbing her head.

"Damn, you're doing a hell of a job," moaned Divine right before releasing.

After Destiny got a warm washcloth to clean him up, they held each other and watched television in bed for a few hours. Then they

Deaubrey Devine

got dressed and went to hang out around the resort.

"I'm sorry about last night," apologized Divine while they were walking.

"I'm sorry, also. It really wasn't that big to me to have sex on the same night as our wedding, but it meant a lot to you," replied Destiny.

"Well, we should come together and talk, not just avoid the situation. If it's something we don't understand thoroughly or if there is something bothering one of us, we should not delay discussing it," explained Divine.

"I hear you, baby. I just didn't feel like being bothered last night," Destiny said.

"Well, I could have put a towel down last night to make love to you, or we could have made love in the shower. That's how horny I was for you last night," laughed Divine.

"Boy, you're a real freak!" screamed Destiny, while smiling.

"I'm kidding," Divine quickly responded.

"Naw, you're not kidding, Freaky D," laughed Destiny.

"On the real, Destiny, just know that I'm trying to expose you to some new and different things, and I want you to do the same," he said, as he grabbed his wife's hand and they walked across the wooden bridge with the calm water flowing underneath.

Destiny snuggled close to her gem. "Okay, baby, I'll try," she replied.

The two enjoyed their evening together and then returned home the next day to begin their married life.

132

CHAPTER 22

After several days of picking up and dropping off Destiny at her aunt's house, Divine grew curious as to why she was leaving her car parked at her friend's house instead of driving it.

"Why is it that I have to pick you up and drop you off when you have a car that is working order?" Divine asked her one day.

"Is that asking too much of you?" asked Destiny, getting smart with Divine.

"Yes, because it's a lot on me when I'm just getting off work and have to come pick you and Desire up and then drop you guys off. Why can't you just move in with me and tell your aunt that you'll still pay your part of the bills for the month?" suggested Divine.

"I'll move in with you in two weeks, but the reason why I'm not driving my car around is because I'm three payments behind on my car note. I've been trying to avoid the repo people that keep calling. They've come to my aunt's house and everything looking for the car. I can't afford to lose my car," explained Destiny.

"Why didn't you say something a long time ago? Why are you keeping something like this a secret?" Divine yelled.

"I didn't want to burden you with my car payment problems, Divine."

"That's not a burden. I'm your husband now and that will affect the both of us. This evening, we need to sit down together and tackle these financial problems we have. Tell your aunt that you're moving in with me so we can start working on us as a family as a whole," said Divine, ending the conversation.

Deciding they needed a bigger place than the apartment which was once Divine's bachelor pad, Divine went to the rental office and expressed that he would have to break his lease. After Divine applied to the apartment complex that Destiny had referred him to, Destiny faxed her information over to be approved so they could take advantage of the apartment's free move-in special for the month. When Divine began to pack his belongings, he threw away all of his magazines and tapes that stimulated his sexual desires, while thinking, *I don't need these anymore because I'm going to be beating me a little something up every night.*

Over the next few days, they both packed and went to pick up the keys to their new apartment. When the weekend arrived, Divine guided the movers with the furniture and big items, while Destiny started to unpack the boxes and decorate the apartment. When Destiny and Divine settled in their apartment, Destiny took Desire over to her aunt's house as Divine anointed the new apartment with holy oil before he went into his new prayer closet to pray to God.

Lord, bless me to be the man you want me to be by following your laws and decrees. Bless me to be obedient to your word so I can treat my family like you want me to as the head. Also, bless me to treat my wife like a real woman and do the best I can to take care of her needs.

When Destiny returned from dropping off Desire, he led his wife in a joint prayer while they walked through the house. Afterwards, they sat down on the couch to discuss the business with their financial future. With a pad and pen in hand, Divine started to budget the figures of both of their incomes combined. While doing so, he noticed that Destiny's finances weren't adding up to the amount she had to payout in bills each month. She owed more per month than she made.

Damn, I wish I would have done this before we got married, Divine thought.

"We need to stop spending money on things we don't necessarily need, and start paying off some of what we owe," Divine said before asking Destiny how was her credit.

"Woo, I think there should be tax cuts for people with bad credit," responded Destiny, as Divine shook his head and smiled.

"Baby, we'll have to average in the rest of the bills when we get our credit reports and budget with these payouts on this pad. Would you mind giving me your paycheck and I give you a certain amount per pay check to live off of? That way, you won't have to worry about any financial issues or bills," proposed Divine as a step toward digging her out of the debt pit she had dug for herself.

"So how much would I get?" asked Destiny, straightening herself up. She wasn't too keen about Divine having control of her money.

"Well, you'll get this amount here," said Divine, circling the amount on the pad.

She felt it was fair, but was curious to see how much Divine would be banking. "So how much you get?" she asked, cutting her eyes.

"Who me?" replied Divine, taken off guard by her question.

"Yeah, you, fool. How much will you get since you make more?"

"I don't know, but any extra I get will go towards us catching up with these bills. Also, we need to put money aside for any emergencies that may come up and for a down payment on a house," Divine replied. "First things first, I'm going to shuffle a few things around so you can get caught up two payments on your car note. I'll figure out something for your other payment, but at least we'll have money left over for this high-ass behind gas and food.

"Dang, Destiny, I can't believe you owe so many people. You could have used your earned income credit to pay them off," he added. "Also, Sugar, it's very important for you to have good credit if you want to be listed on the mortgage for the house when we purchase one. I'm in the upper 600's with my credit score. Tomorrow, I'll go add your name to the jewelry account as well as all the rest of my accounts to help build your credit because all of them will be paid on time," Divine informed her, as he closed the pad and stood up.

"Even your bank account?" asked Destiny.

Divine hesitated, while thinking, *Hell naw! You can't even manage your own bills. What the hell I look like giving you full access to my account?*

"Why do you need to be on my account?" questioned Divine.

"Well, I have to wait a year before I can reopen my account with my bank from all my bounced checks and late fees," explained Destiny, as Divine thought, *See? Hell to the naw. I don't have 'duck' written on my face.*

"I'll tell you what. I'll open a joint account for us that we can use to pay our bills out of, and I'll just keep my account separate."

"So you're telling me that you can have access to all my finances, but I can't have access to yours? Is that what you're saying?"

"Destiny, I'm just trying to make this work for the both of us," Divine replied in an exhausted voice, not wanting to argue with her.

"And how do I know you're going to do the right thing with the money? What if you leave me and keep all the money we save?"

"Why are you even thinking like that and we just got married?" Divine said, raising his voice about Destiny's crazy way of thinking. "Let's just try it out and not derail the train," said Divine, as the two began the plan.

One day, after a few weeks of not eating $15 plus meals at work every day, the frustrated Destiny was approached by Faith who was on her way out the door.

"Destiny, have you been taking care of business on the real estate schooling? Everything is in the making and things should be popping off really soon," Faith said, while sitting her laptop case on the countertop.

"I may have to put that on hold because Divine and I have a budget and we're trying to buy a house soon," explained Destiny, as she broke down the whole situation to Faith about Divine and the accounts.

"Are you cuckoo? That is a bad idea for you guys to have separate accounts. Girl, that's the perfect outlet for a man to cheat and do whatever without you ever knowing about it," giggled Faith.

"I know. I actually have talked it over with a few friends and have come to the conclusion that Divine is hiding something with the finances," replied Destiny, feeling pushed over.

"You better handle you biz. Well, I'll see you later. I have to rush to this meeting," Faith said, as she grabbed her bag and walked off.

Later that evening, Destiny confronted Divine with her apprehension regarding the budget plan he had set forth.

"Divine, I feel like I'm powerless and without a voice in this relationship. I've talked with my friends, and they all say I would be a fool to go along with your budgeting plan. To be honest, I seriously think it's just too secretive for me," voiced Destiny.

"Destiny, first of all, you're grown. Be a woman and make your own decisions. I'm pretty sure the people you talked to don't know about your debt and credit. We just have to believe in God and trust that God will bring us on through financially. We're not struggling or wanting for nothing. We're just on a strict budget to correct what hole we've dug ourselves in," explained Divine, as Destiny became angry.

"Well, will our stupid budget allow me to go back to school?"

"Of course, just let me know so we can plan for it and put it in the budget." replied Divine.

"I'm tired of you saying trust God for this and that. I shouldn't have to trust God to eat lunch at work and believe God for personal spending money. Unless we can have one account where I know where all the money is going, I want no parts of your budgeting system. It's not fair for you to know all my transactions and I not know about yours."

Divine became heated. "Look, we have to stick to our goal to pay off our debts and save. We can't afford to splurge!" he yelled.

"Divine, why can't we just live a little? By God, you have to treat yourself every now and then. Those bills are going to be there regardless," responded Destiny in disagreement.

"But in order to meet our goals faster, we need to stick to the plan."

"Forget it! I need a husband, and not someone acting like my father," spat Destiny, before storming out of the house.

After she left, Divine stood in the middle of the room feeling empty. *What am I suppose to do as her husband and we don't have a pot to piss in or a window to throw it out?*

Over the next few days, Divine convinced Destiny that they should budget for her to go back to school, while Destiny expressed she would be keeping her paycheck and handling her own personal finances. To avoid an argument, Divine handed over all of Destiny's bills from out of the bible he kept them in. He then told her that he would pay all the bills if she could just take care of the lights and credit card bills. He also told her that he would pay half on Desire's daycare.

During the week, Destiny and Faith had lunch together.

"Faith, thanks for treating me to lunch. You know, Divine isn't pleasing me mentally as a head and provider. I'm to the point where I don't even want to lay down with him to have sex," Destiny vented.

"Fuck him. Hold out. You have to feel him with your heart and not just your pussy all the time. Work towards your schooling and do you," Faith replied, as the two women high-fived each other. "Girl, get your ass a drink," laughed Faith.

"Well, I don't drink anymore since my accident in college," Destiny responded.

"You have to loosen up a little bit. I'm going to treat you to a girl's night out next week. When will you be free?" asked Faith.

"It's hard to get a babysitter during the week."

"Well, I can't do it on the weekend. But is there any way you can sneak out during Wednesday's church service after singing?"

"I actually can," replied Destiny, agreeing with the good suggestion.

"Well, use your head and don't even tell the hubby because he will start questioning you. Hell, you have to start doing you until things are modified for Destiny and Desire," educated Faith.

During lunch, Faith convinced Destiny not to purchase a house with Divine if her name wouldn't be included on the deed because of her bad credit. So, when Destiny went home, she expressed to Divine that she wanted to renew their twelve-month instead of buying a house that her name wouldn't be on.

"Baby, we need equity to help us financially, and since we're married now, your name would still be added to the deed," Divine explained, as he began to grow tired of the fighting.

"Well, I don't care. Besides, I want to rent until I pay off all my debt," Destiny replied, not budging.

How are you going to be able to do all this with no plan? This is going to take forever, he thought, growing fatigued from arguing.

"Okay, we'll wait until you get your credit together," replied Divine, giving in, while committing to help pay off the small things on her credit report in hopes of speeding up the process of them buying their first home together.

CHAPTER 23

As Destiny found herself in a bad position with her finances again from overspending, she went submissively to Divine, humbled herself, apologized, and asked her husband if they could work together on their budgeting system. Needless to say, Divine was all too eager to get things back on track. However, after only a few days, Destiny got another attitude with Divine because he wouldn't give her any extra money for her to eat deep fried crabs at lunch the next day from a seafood spot near her job. So, Destiny decided to take her anger out on Divine by not speaking to him and driving separate cars to choir rehearsal that night.

The next day, Faith treated Destiny to lunch at the seafood restaurant. While talking and having a few drinks, Destiny began to open up to Faith about her life experiences and the problems plaguing her marriage, especially in regards to finances.

"You should call Divine and have him call and check his account with you on the phone to see if there have been any transactions on his card within the last few days since he claims he has nothing to hide," Faith suggested, knowing that Destiny would discover he had been paying her cell phone bill, although Divine had no idea that the money was being taken out of his account.

After paying the tab and leaving a tip, Faith led Destiny to her car where she could place the call to Divine without having to deal with all the noise distractions inside the restaurant. Once inside the car, Destiny dialed Divine's number and requested he check his account using three-way calling. Not knowing what had led to Destiny's strange request, he didn't hesitate to oblige since he had nothing to hide when it came to their finances. During the automated recording speaking the most recent transactions for the month, it was revealed that there were automatic withdrawals issued to Nextel Cellular. Destiny found this to be a strange charge, especially since Divine's cell phone carrier was Sprint. When Destiny called him on this, he quickly responded by saying there must have been some error on the bank's part and that he would have to call and have that issue addressed. He knew the charge must have been a repeated withdrawal from his account from when he did Faith the one-time favor of paying her cell phone bill. However, there was no way he could tell his wife that he had known Faith well enough to do such a favor. She would never understand.

"There is something fishy about all this, Divine," Destiny replied. "This is exactly why I didn't want to go along with all this budgeting crap," she said before hanging up, while Faith quickly played the part of a good friend and calmed her down.

Immediately, Divine called his bank to cancel the debit card and have a new one issued.

Wednesday evening, Destiny drove to church service in her own car and took her place in the choir stands, with her friends in the choir asking if everything was okay between her and Divine. She replied they were fine and that he wasn't feeling well. After the choir sang and the tithe and offerings were collected, the choir members were released to sit in the congregation with the rest of the church, while Divine looked for his wife to come sit with him, but she never did.

Instead, Destiny decided to leave out of church undetected and go to a nearby restaurant to meet with Faith. As she departed from the doors of the church, she placed a call to her aunt's phone, which she knew would be turned off during service, and left a message for her to pick Desire up from daycare.

When Destiny arrived, she let go of her inhibitions and allowed Faith to treat her to a few 2-1 drinks. Faith sipped very lightly while watching her colleague get loose. At that point, Faith asked Destiny to accompany her back at her home for a few more drinks.

With Destiny staggering into Faith's apartment very muddled by the liquor, Faith played like she was just as tipsy, while taking Destiny into her room.

"Destiny, are you down for a little girl play?" asked Faith.

"What are you talking about?" whispered Destiny in a slurred speech.

140

She felt Faith kiss her neck and ears before palming her breast to begin licking and sucking on her breast that she had pulled from the confines of Destiny's shirt. With Faith taking full advantage of Destiny, she tongued her deeply while removing Destiny's articles of clothing. Not putting up any resistance, Destiny soon found her clitoris being rubbed by Faith's two middle fingers that rotated slowly on her hot spot. She moaned while releasing tension, as Faith started plunging her finger in and out of her in a steady, fast pace.

"Let go and be free. Let's finish our girl's night the right way," whispered Faith, before placing finger that was soaked with Destiny's juices into Destiny's mouth.

"I'm nervous. I've never been with a woman," Destiny replied, as she watched Faith undress.

"This is my first time trying this, too. But let's just experiment and get lost in our own world. Baby, I want you to spread your legs eagle like some Lamborghini doors," directed Faith in a sexy voice, taking control by lifting Destiny's legs off the bed and into the air.

While Faith moved her head from side to side and her tongue ring rubbed against Destiny's pearl tongue, Destiny moaned with intense pleasure as her juices flowed freely.

"I want to introduce you to my friends the two-headed monster and Big Daddy," smiled Faith, as she rubbed Destiny's leg that trembled as her body quivered from the orgasm. "See the nana doesn't taste so bad. Do it ma?" giggled Faith, then wrapped her mouth around one end of the double dildo while lying on Destiny's chest and placing the other end in her mouth.

After a few minutes of watching Destiny work her mouth on the dildo, Faith had the desire to please her through penetration. So, she put away the 18-inch latex toy and strapped the titanic to the leather G-string harness, which was attached to her lower body.

Destiny found enough strength left in her body after releasing the built-up pressure to ask Faith, "What are you doing?"

"I want to try something new. Just lay back and let me take your body where it has never been before," replied Faith, as she slipped the head of Big Daddy into Destiny, causing her to spring off the bed. "Damn, Divine must have a short-ass fishing rod if your ocean can't take this," commented Faith, while trying again to ease inside of Destiny inch by inch. "Tell me you like King Kong!" shouted Faith to see if Destiny was enjoying it and not just doing it by force.

"I like it," winced Destiny, while taking the pain of Faith going inside of her a little deeper.

"Come on, talk to me. Make those tight, wet muscles squeeze poppa. Come on, Destiny, make Big Daddy tap out because he's choking it to death," Faith demanded, as she started pounding Destiny at a faster pace.

"I like it!" shouted Destiny, her body rocking from the thrusts Faith were delivering. "It feels good. Oh shit, it feels good!" repeated Destiny.

"Say Big Daddy!" yelled Faith, as she began to have no mercy and started banging Destiny without mercy.

"Big Daddy...Shit, Big Daddy!" Destiny screamed, while matching Faith thrust for thrust.

"Can I get an Amen that King Kong is good," said Faith, sensing that Destiny was about to release.

"Amen! Amen! Ooohh, Amen!" Destiny cried out, as her eyes rolled back in her head and her body convulsed in the bed.

Meanwhile Divine was upset at Destiny for disappearing after singing in the choir instead of joining him in the congregation. When he caught up with Destiny's aunt after the service, he learned that Destiny had left her a message to pick up Desire. However, her aunt had plans to meet with the usher board. Divine found it strange that Destiny left church without telling anyone, but not wanting Destiny's aunt to be inconvenienced, he told her that he would take Desire with him. While driving, Divine called Destiny's phone several times, but didn't get an answer. Once home, Divine fed Desire, bathed her, and then read her a bedtime story. He then got on his knees to pray with her, as he had Desire repeat the Lord's Prayer after him, before putting her to bed.

Back at Faith's house, while Destiny was passed out in a drunken coma, Faith took Destiny's keys off the dresser and went to the hardware store in the plaza up the street from her house to make a copy of her apartment key. Not long after Faith returned, Destiny woke up.

"Destiny," Faith said, "I hope that what happened between us will remain between us. Please don't go telling anyone."

"Trust, our secret is safe with me," replied Destiny, kind of embarrassed by what she had taken part in. "It's weird, but I really don't look at you the same," she added, while staring at Faith. "I feel like you have taught me something new."

"Girl, hush, it just happened between us. It could never be because neither one of us get down like that on a regular," laughed Faith.

"I know, but I did enjoy it," Destiny divulged, smiling. "Well, let me get home. I'm sure I'm going to get interrogated about where I've been by Divine," she said, while gathering her belongings.

Upon entering the house, Destiny walked straight to Desire's room to check on her and give her a kiss before going into her room, passing Divine without speaking.

"Destiny, where in the hell have you been?" shouted Divine.

"Oh, are we cursing now? I've never heard you curse," laughed Destiny.

"Hell is in the bible. Now, where have you been? You never go out," Divine replied.

"That's the problem. I had a girl's night out. I'm tired of being sheltered," Destiny responded, then walked out of the room and went to take a shower.

Lord, protect our mind as the enemy comes to kill, steal, and destroy while he tries to attack our minds first, prayed Divine.

Once Destiny finished showering, she stuck her head inside the bedroom and told Divine good night before disappearing into Desire's room.

I can't believe this girl, Divine thought, as he hopped off the bed, followed her into Desire's room, and cut on the light. "Do you want to pray, because I can't take this tension between us?" asked Divine, feeling overpowered.

"Naw, I'm straight. I'll say my own prayer. Now, could you please cut the light off before you wake up Desire? Thank you, sweetie."

The family who prays together stays together, and this is not looking good at all for my family, Divine thought as he turned off the light and retreated back to the lonely marital bedroom.

143

CHAPTER 24

"Do you want to go look for a few house later today?" asked Divine the next day while on his way home from work.

"I already told you, Divine, that I don't feel comfortable with purchasing a house with you right now. I already expressed that I want to continue renting, so why must you push the issue?"

"Destiny, come on. I'm exhausted and I really don't feel like arguing with you."

"No argument from me. Just know that I will not be accompanying you if you decide to go out searching for a house."

"Fine," Divine said before hanging up.

After taking a nap, Divine went to look at several homes with a real estate agent, and then narrowed the homes down to the two he liked. The agent informed Divine that he would have a lot of equity in the properties once the construction of the park and community center in the area was finished. Divine told the agent that he would make his decision after his wife had a chance to take a look at the properties.

Excited about his big move in his marriage, he called up Hope to share the news. He missed sharing conversations and good times with her, especially when he couldn't talk to his wife. When Divine called Hope, she congratulated him and expressed her happiness for his family's life-changing accomplishment.

"I'm proud of you. That's good that you bring something to the table and offer something as a man. A lot of men are out here just looking for handouts instead of being a provider," Hope said.

Divine laughed. "Alright, that's enough about your man. All men aren't like that," Divine replied, speaking up for some brothers.

"I'm serious. Some men are just lazy, sorry individuals who do not want to go out and work to get what they want. Then you have the ones who are addicted to living that fast life and making that fast money, with the end result being jail or death," voiced Hope, as they continued talking about the rise and fall of Black men.

"You know, Hope, I'm very thankful for you and just these few minutes of having a peaceful conversation. I don't understand how Destiny and I hear the same word at church and she doesn't apply it to our daily living situations," shared Divine.

"Just hang in there. God's got it. He'll bless your sacred marriage," replied Hope after listening to Divine's yearning for change.

"I sure hope so. I'm putting my trust and belief in God for a miracle to happen soon. Hope, sometimes I get so excited to see Destiny, but when I see her, she gives me attitude. It always seems like someone let all the air out of me," sighed Divine.

"Divine, I miss our high school days when we were together. Do you regret what we did at all?" asked Hope, hoping to put a smile Divine's face.

"No, I don't regret them at all," laughed Divine.

"I always wanted you to be my husband, but things turned out different."

"Yeah, and they did in a big way," exhaled Divine wearily. The two enjoyed talking for a while, reminiscing about the past before hanging up.

When Destiny returned home later that evening with shopping bags in each hand, Divine told her that he had picked out two houses, and explained about the instant equity they would have if they purchased one of them. He then told her that he would put down the payment required to start the process of buying their first house if she was happy after seeing it.

Divine felt he was blessing his wife with good news, but the shit hit the fan when Destiny became furious.

"Divine, I never thought you could be this rude to me," Destiny said, while placing the shopping bags on the bed. "How could you do such a thing after I made it clear that I didn't want to buy?" yelled Destiny.

After Divine tried to explain the pluses of buying a house while the market was low to gain financial stability, she replied, "You always want to take control and do it your damn way. That's not right for you to do that. You could have at least waited on me to see if I wanted to go at a later time!" shouted Destiny.

"You said you didn't want to buy a house, and that crap isn't right when I'm trying to be a head for our family and lead us in the right direction. We're just giving money away year in and year out by renting," rationalized Divine.

"You just don't get it, Divine! This is exact reason why I've broken the spiritual covenant between you, I, and God by sleeping with someone else!" she screamed.

When Destiny spoke those words, Divine's heart stopped and his mouth became dry. He immediately had flashbacks to when Precious would cheat on her husband with him, and wondered if this was karma coming back to haunt him.

"Destiny, let's just get the bible and pray," replied Divine, not knowing any other way to respond to her revelation.

"What? Are you an idiot? God don't tell you how to brush your teeth or tie your shoes. You need to do something about it," demanded Destiny, while looking at Divine with a puzzled and reckless stare.

"Alright, I forgive you. No one's perfect; everyone has flaws," Divine replied, swallowing hard in a attempt to hold back his tears.

Walking off, Divine retreated to his prayer closet, fell flat on his face, and wept to God for strength.

Lord! God knows I'm trying to do everything you want me to do in this marriage. I've never cursed her out, hit her, or disrespected her. I don't know what to do other than stand still and tolerate the reason you have me here. I'm crying out to you to make a way out of no way.

After calling off from work, he lied in a puddle of tears before falling asleep while praying for direction.

CHAPTER 25

Over the next few weeks, Destiny tried to shuffle things around so she could have more money in her pocket and wouldn't have to be dependent on Divine. While she sat at work scribbling a financial plan out on a piece of paper, Faith approached her desk.

"Destiny, what are you doing writing all those numbers?" questioned Faith.

"Girl, I'm trying to find a way to save money until I get my income tax check. I can't wait to get that earned income credit. You know I'm in need right now, but I'm very skeptical of asking people for things because they tend to throw it back up in your face when they help you. It often tends to come back to haunt you in the end."

"Well, good luck, girl, but you do know that your filing status changed when you got married, right? As a result, you probably won't get as much back on your return as you did when you filed as being single and head of household," Faith explained, breaking the news to Destiny, whose mouth dropped.

"What?" replied Destiny, as she sat in disbelief.

"Yeah, girl, all that shit changes when you say 'I do'. Your problems become his problems and vice versa. So, girl, you better use what you have to your advantage, and ride that cobra to capacity in order to get the things you need in your marriage," Faith suggested.

"I may have to do just that, but in a few weeks. I'm too mad now," chuckled Destiny.

"Alright, well, I'll talk to you later," Faith responded, while walking off.

For most of the afternoon, Destiny surfed the internet to research how her tax status would change by being married. What she found out did not make her happy, to say the least.

Upon arriving home, Divine greeted Destiny with a surprise, which was a nice diamond watch he had charged to their jewelry account. He hoped that the gift would lessen the tension between the two of them. However, when Destiny accepted the gift, she gave Divine an evil stare, while looking at him with confusion in her eyes.

"You just don't get it, do you?" said Destiny in a curt tone.

"Nothing seems to make you happy," replied Divine in a fatigued voice.

"I just found out that I can't get earned income credit on my tax returns, and I was looking forward to having that money to help pay for my education when I go back to school," Destiny explained, worrying about her future.

"Honey, you will be able to go back to school. Don't worry. I'll work all the extra hours that I need for us to be able to accomplish our goals. We're one now. Just break your husband off a little bit of that honey love every now and then," smiled Divine, as he walked towards Destiny to hug her.

She pushed him back hard. "You're just saying that to make me feel good. You're too direct and in your box to do that," replied Destiny sarcastically, as she thought, *I'd rather receive the guaranteed money from the earned income credit.*

"Why did you even get married to me if you were not ready?" questioned Divine, not understanding the reasons for her attitude. "Maybe God is trying to elevate us to another level. We're fine. We just need to read our word a little more," said Divine.

"Why you always throw God up in my ears like brass symbols? What is Divine going to do to make it happen?" replied Destiny, her nasty voice escalading.

"What more can I do? You don't want for anything. You just try and live for the day and not tomorrow. I'm trying to plan now and help us move on up like the Jefferson's. I sit up here and listen to you complain because I want you to talk to me about the circumstances and be upfront with your husband!"

"You disgust me. I've fallen out of love with you," replied Destiny, while cutting her eyes and frowning her face up.

Divine looked at her not knowing how to respond as millions of things ran through his mind in a few seconds.

"Baby, let's just get counseling. Now is a time when we have to pull together and not have a tug a war," Divine said in response to his wife's words that shredded his heart to pieces.

"Counseling is just someone else in our business."

What else can I do? What exactly am I here for? This is my wife telling me this, thought Divine as he replied, "You're wrong and hurtful for those words."

Without another word, Destiny walked off to go in Desire's room, where she locked herself up until Divine went to work that night.

The next morning, Destiny announced that she and Desire would be moving out.

"Destiny, a separation is not going to solve anything, but instead allow a lot of ungodly thoughts to torment our minds," explained Divine, while following his wife back and forth to her car as she loaded her and Desire's belongings into the trunk before getting in the car and driving off, leaving him standing there with a broken heart.

After pleading and contacting Destiny on the phone, along with popping up over her aunt's house, she returned home because she had no privacy. However, upon coming back, she boldly told Divine that her legs were closed and for him not to expect any sex.

As the days went by, Divine relied on visiting X-rated websites in order to satisfy himself sexually. Before signing off, he would make sure to erase the search engine history so Destiny would not discover what he had been doing.

One day while driving down his street, Lemon Head's voice rang clear in his head. *If you want to cheat on your wife, call me?* After driving halfway to his old apartment complex, he thought hard about disrespecting his vows he made to God, but really didn't want to be like Danny Boy and cheat on his wife. Divine then pulled over into the parking lot of a nearby plaza up the street from his old apartment.

"Fuck! Why aren't you answering the damn phone?" said Divine, hitting the steering wheel hard after Lemon Head didn't answer her phone.

After having no luck with Lemon Head, Divine called Destiny to apologize for just leaving the house.

"What's up?" said Destiny, answering the phone in a nonchalant voice.

"Look, Destiny, I'm tired of going through this bullshit. All this stupid shit is draining me emotionally. We're going to have to talk this through and get help," replied Divine, stepping outside of his Christianity for a moment.

"Oh, boy, I thought you actually wanted something. I'll talk to you later. I'm busy looking at Desire color in her coloring book," Destiny responded in a calm voice as she hung up the phone.

Something is really not connecting with my wife, Divine thought.

As he pulled out of the parking lot, he turned up the gospel music he had playing in an attempt to keep the enemy from taking control of his mind and allowing him to make the mistake of giving into his temptation of the flesh.

CHAPTER 26

"Well, good morning, baby," Destiny said, the morning of her birthday as she ambushed Divine at the door when he returned from work, giving him a hug and a kiss on the cheek.

"Good morning and happy birthday. How's the birthday girl?" smiled Divine.

"She's good. Now where is her birthday present? She's not that picky when it comes to some things, but she needs her surprise gift on her birthday, which is now," said Destiny, unreserved in her request.

Divine thought, *Damn, she's more straightforward than she was a year ago.*

"Well, I have these beautiful roses for you now, and a special evening planned. So, come straight home," replied Divine, smiling.

"Alright, I'll see you around six," Destiny said, as she left to take Desire to the daycare.

That evening, Divine took Destiny to a nice, expensive restaurant with dim lighting. During dinner, they enjoyed great conversation and good laughs.

"I hope you enjoyed your birthday dinner," Divine said, as they were walking back to the car.

"Yes, I did. Thank you so much. It's been a while since we have had an evening to ourselves."

"I'm glad," Divine replied. "I love you, Destiny, but I think it's messed up that you hold out at times on the sex when things don't go your way," laughed Divine, while looking over at Destiny who was giggling.

"Well, you won't have to worry about me holding out tonight. I'm horny and don't feel like playing any games. I'm ready for you to ride this donkey and work this monkey tonight," replied Destiny. "So

151

are we going to have fun tonight? I want this to be a birthday I won't forget," Destiny added, wanting to have a wild and adventurous night.

"So what's up, baby? What did you have in mind?" asked Divine, perking up and becoming curious.

"Well, tonight I just want to feel free and let go for my birthday. I want to get buck wild. What do you think about that?"

"Hell, I'm down for it. I haven't been saved all my life, and I really would like to see that other side of you having fun. So, do you want to go out to a club?" asked Divine.

"No, we don't have to do that. We can stop by the liquor store and get something to enjoy in the comfort of our own home."

"What would you like to drink?" Divine asked.

"Hennessey!" shouted Destiny, as Divine looked at her thinking, *How in the hell does she know about Hennessey.*

While making sure to drive to the liquor store on the other side of town to make sure no one from the church saw him purchasing liquor, he asked Destiny, "What do you want to chase the liquor with?"

"Nothing," replied Destiny.

Divine just gave Destiny a puzzled look and thought, *What the hell? I don't even drink that stuff...let alone would I attempt to drink it straight.*

Once Divine returned to the car with the bottle in the brown paper bag, Destiny wasted no time cracking it open and turning it straight up to her mouth. She coughed and gagged from its potency.

"Are you okay?" smiled Divine.

"Yeah, I'm okay. It just burned as it traveled down the pipe," replied Destiny, with her red, glazed eyes before turning up the bottle again.

"Alright, now! You shouldn't be doing that bottle like that," Divine laughed.

"Here, you turn it up," giggled Destiny to get Divine involved in the action.

"Man, this splash is too strong for me. It's been a minute since I've slushed," hissed Divine after taking a drink and giving the bottle back to Destiny. "Man, we're going to be fucked up."

"Well, I'm going to party like it's my birthday. Oh, wait! It is my birthday. Now let me hit another sip of this strong splash," she replied, taking a drink as they pulled up to the apartment. Before walking inside, Destiny drunk dialed Faith to share how drunk she was and how she was enjoying her night.

While Divine was using the restroom, Destiny slipped into a matching bra and thong set.

"Got damn, baby!" shouted Divine in awe as his friend rose from the dead upon Destiny entering the living room.

He pulled Destiny close as the quiet storm played on the radio, then he laid her on the couch and stuck his tongue in Destiny's cotton candy as she moaned.

"Baby, I love you," said Divine between the passionate kissing, breathing hard, and rubbing all over each other's bodies.

Destiny pushed Divine on the floor so she could swallow Divine's massive piece like a whale. She pleased her man with a few new tricks, as Divine's eyes rolled back into his head. Next, she positioned herself on top of him and rode him like the dick was going out of style.

"Dang, baby, where is all this freakiness coming from?" smiled Divine, as Destiny turned around to ride Divine backwards. "Man, what the fuck has gotten into you?" he said, while trying to hold on to her waist as he jerked.

"I just love you so much, even though you upset me sometimes. My kitty is always purring for you," replied Destiny, as Divine gripped her butt cheeks.

"Hold on. I want to try something new and kinky." Destiny jumped up off of him and soon returned with her new sex toy, The Rabbit. Handing it over to Divine, he took control and placed the vibrating toy on her clit.

"Yes, big daddy!" shouted Destiny. "Oh shit, Big Daddy Divine. Be my papi and spank me if you want. Baby, it feels too good right now. Don't stop. Please get freakier with me. Do whatever you please. I want you to arch this up and hit it from the back," added Destiny, as she flipped over and placed two pillows under her stomach.

Divine followed her command and started long stroking her from the rear.

"Here, put it in my butt," said Destiny, as she gave him the lubricant. After oiling up his wife's other hole, he eased into her entrance.

"Damn, baby, that feels good. Oh, baby, I'm coming," Destiny panted, as Divine smiled.

"This was some freaky stuff we were doing, Destiny," said Divine after they finished showering.

Soon they were both sleep.

Peeping through the blinds, Faith could see the two of them knocked out in a deep, drunken sleep. As Divine slept on his back in his white long john top and bottoms in the pitch dark apartment, Faith's obsession with Divine grew bold.

If I get caught, oh well. I need to try and get me some while the both of them are passed out, thought Faith as she walked to her car to get their apartment key, then crept into the apartment to strategize a plan to climb on Divine.

As she saw Divine sprawled out all over the bed and Destiny lying next to him, Faith inserted her cervical sponge and positioned Divine's body in a letter 'Y'.

Please don't wake up, thought Faith, while scooting Destiny's body to the foot of the bed, positioning her on her back with her head hanging off the bed and her butt sitting on Divine's shins.

As Faith stepped over Destiny's legs that were spread to face Divine, she started easing down his bottoms. As she got them halfway past his thighs, Divine began to wake up.

"Baby," whispered Divine in a quiet voice, while attempting to raise his heavy head.

Shit, what the fuck am I going to do, thought Faith, freezing in her tracks. "Shhh," said Faith, as she pushed Divine's chest back down and wrapped her lips around his manhood. "Baby, let your wife finish up her birthday the right way," whispered Faith, pretending to be Destiny.

Not noticing the difference in the quiet voice, Divine smiled and laid his spinning head back on the bed.

After pleasing Divine for a few minutes, Faith turned around to Destiny, who was passed out, and ran her hand down the right side of Destiny's face.

"I can't forget about the birthday girl. A family that makes love together, stays together," smiled Faith before unleashing her tongue to treat Destiny, while sitting on Divine's stiff shaft and riding him until she had a mini orgasm to complete the birthday threesome.

When Faith finished, she went in the bathroom and threw her cervical sponge in the trash. Before leaving, she repositioned Destiny on her side, pulled Divine's bottoms back up, and eased out of the house.

CHAPTER 27

The next morning, Destiny went in the bathroom to take a shower. When she finished showering, she stood in front of the mirror to lotion her body and to comb her hair.

Oh Lord, let me get this hair out the sink before I get thirty lashes from Divine, she thought, while cleaning the hair from out of the sink. When she walked over to the trash can to throw the tissue and hair away, she noticed the cervical sponge.

"Well fuck me running backwards. Divine, what in the fuck is this?" shouted Destiny, as Divine rushed into the bathroom.

"What's up, baby?" Divine asked, while Destiny pointed in the trash can.

"Don't fucking 'baby' me. What's up with this shit?" yelled the furious Destiny, as she began to cry. "What is that?" she screamed, while Divine stood puzzled as to why there was a used cervical sponge in their bathroom trash can when he hadn't cheated. "Look, a mature man wouldn't take a grown woman through little boy games," bawled Destiny.

"Well, did you know that blasphemy is one of the greatest sins?" Divine shot back.

"Whatever, you cheating bitch. Someone told me that I was stupid for letting you cheat on me with your so-called cousin before I even got myself into this marriage."

"I can't really say what I want to say because I'm saved, but you better be glad God has changed me. I'm not going to sit up here and take the blame for some shit that you're planning. If you're unhappy and want to continue to cheat on me, haul ass and leave. Please, Destiny, let me know right now where you stand in this relationship. I'm tired of these firestorms," replied Divine, tired of the up and downs of their marriage.

"I don't know what to believe happened, but with this cervical sponge as physical evidence, I do not believe anything you say. I just can't believe you're trying to switch shit around on me when I'm just coming to you to get the truth on whose is this. Damn, I wish I had a lie detector test right now!" shouted Destiny, as she cut her eyes to the ceiling before reaching in the trash can to take out the sponge with some tissue to hold it up in the air so Divine could see it.

Divine stood mad as he looked at the used cervical sponge. His heart began to melt as his mind made him believe this was her way of trying to cover up her infidelity again.

"You're a fucking fraud!" shouted Divine in a nasty tone, while looking his wife directly in her eyes.

"What the fuck did you just say?"

"You heard me. I'm not repeating shit," replied Divine.

Enraged, Destiny threw the cervical sponge at Divine, hitting him on the side of his neck as he turned his face away.

In a burning rage, he picked the sponge up with his bare hands and threw it back at her, hitting her in the face. "Man, calm the fuck down," said Divine, as Destiny rushed him.

"Naw, bitch! You're not going to sit up here and disrespect me with your distrustful ass!" replied Destiny, as Divine held her pinned down to the bed.

"I love you, Destiny, and I'm clear and upfront with my credibility. I still loved you the same after you told me you broke the spiritual covenant between you, me, and God and that you've fallen out of love with me. That shit hurts. But I realize, with God's grace, that it's important to cherish your mate whether it is or isn't the way you want them to be," cried Divine, as Destiny became still while listening to him.

"Now can I get up?" Destiny yelled.

"Man, Destiny, don't hit me. I've never cursed you out, disrespected you, or hit you. So, please, keep your hands to yourself," he stated before allowing her to get up off the bed.

"You know what? God gives you a spirit of discernment, which is one of my strong gifts, and he keeps telling me that you're not the man that I need to be with. I'm filing for a divorce tomorrow and moving back to my aunt's."

"I think what we really need to do is go to counseling and make this marriage work," Divine replied, knowing that her leaving would not be a solution.

"You can go all you want. I'm out!" Destiny replied, and then started packing her clothes.

Over the next several weeks, Divine spent a lot of time saying silent prayers at work and praying in his prayer closet at home. He continued to fast for direction in his marriage as he listened for God's voice.

When Hope called Divine, he shared with her about him and Destiny's separation and how he was feeling awful.

"Well, don't feel like you're the only one in a bad relationship. I work hard, come home to wash clothes, cook for him, and he still gives me his ass to kiss. I'm a real good woman, Divine," expressed Hope.

"Yeah, I know you are," Divine replied, finding it hard to understand how her dude could act a fool with such a good girl.

"I have no time for games. I've wasted years by moving up here away from my family to this city with him and he won't even work. I can't be in a relationship where I date a guy for fifteen years and end up not becoming his wife. But, see, your situation is different, Divine. You're married, and you know how a marriage is. You have to take the good with the bad. Just hang in there and God will bless you very soon. I know he will," Hope said to encourage her friend.

"You're right. I'm just not use to feeling this bad all the time. I don't regret being married at all. I just take this as a major growing and learning experience. I just need a backbone and supportive system in this whole deal."

"It will come in due season. Just hang in there," replied Hope to perk Divine up.

A few days later, Divine received a call from Cherish, informing him that Uncle Earl was in the hospital. He was not doing well, and the doctors had given him only days to live. Immediately, he called Destiny to ask if she would go to the hospital with him to visit Uncle Earl. However, Destiny refused. She expressed that she hoped he would be okay and that she would pray for him, but since they were separated, she didn't feel comfortable with being around his family, especially during a somber time like the one present. Still, Divine provided her with Uncle Earl's phone number and room number at the hospital in case she decided she wanted to call or visit him.

After hanging up with Destiny, he called Hope to inform her of his uncle being hospitalized, and then placed a call to Uncle Earl.

"Uncle Earl! What's up, champ? Are you okay?"

"Yes, sonny, I'm okay," replied the strong and hard fighting Uncle Earl.

"Unc, do you need anything before I come visit you?" asked Divine, being thoughtful.

"Yes, sonny, you can actually bring me a few things of that...ahh...cranberry juice. The old man needs to stay clean on the inside," giggled Uncle Earl. "Hold on," he said, as he began coughing loud and wheezing.

"I'll be there shortly," replied Divine.

Meanwhile as Divine was visiting with his uncle, Hope called her boss to cancel all her appointments for the next few days and scheduled a flight to Atlanta so she could be there as a friend for Divine.

As Divine sat alone with his uncle and held his hand, Uncle Earl said, "I just want to get out of this place, Divine. I don't like it here."

"Just stay strong, Unc. We're praying that you have a speedy recovery," smiled Divine.

"Well, sonny, when it's your time to go, it's your time to go. And when that time comes for me, I need you to be business minded and carry on my legacy. I want you to take charge and carry on everything I taught you about blessing others and creating wealth for your kids someday," beamed Uncle Earl, even though excruciating pain shot through his body.

"I will, Uncle Earl," Divine assured him.

When Uncle Earl began coughing, Divine got up to pour him some cranberry juice and the weak elderly man took a few sips.

"Thank you," said Uncle Earl after closing his eyes to swallow. "So how's my boy's marriage going?"

"Look, Uncle, if you don't want to clock out sooner than you have to, we'd better leave that subject alone," laughed Divine.

"Well, I don't know both sides of the story, but Destiny has called almost the whole family to talk about you cheating with other women in your home and saying that you have neglected your family's needs by trying to pay other people's bills. You know, Divine, you shouldn't do your wife like that. That's wrong in God's eyes," said Uncle Earl, letting Divine know that his act were ungodly.

"That's not true, Uncle. You know I wasn't raised like that. I'm a firm believer that family is first under God," Divine said, growing angry, while thinking, *I can't believe she's been calling my family with that stupid bullshit.*

"Why are you getting upset?" asked Uncle Earl.

"Uncle, it's really not the time. You're too sick," Divine replied.

"If now isn't the time to talk to me, when will the time be with me only having days to live?" questioned Uncle Earl.

After Divine finished telling his uncle about the continuous downward spiral of his marriage, he added, "But, even though this marriage is starting to cause me to have a nervous breakdown, I'm trying to hold on to the vows I've made to God by not leaving. I just wish I could have back the woman I first met," replied Divine, who loved his wife.

"Divine, that's true, but ask yourself if you want to wake up to hell for the next fifty to sixty years of your life, or would you rather wake up to peace, joy, and happiness for the next fifty to sixty years. That's an important question you have to ask yourself when you're young. God isn't always in the middle of some of the things we create," Uncle Earl wisely informed his nephew.

"Well, that sure puts a lot of things in perspective," replied Divine.

"Just keep God first and pray over all things. It will work out in your favor in the end," Uncle Earl assured him.

That evening, Hope called Divine while he was at work.

"What's up, Divine? What are you doing?"

"I'm just at the site working," replied Divine, as he held the phone to his ear with the help of his shoulder, while guiding the cleaning machine.

"It's a shame how people decide to go to work even when they have someone who has come in town to see them," teased Hope.

"What are you talking about?" Divine asked, confused by her statement.

"Boy, I've come in town to be here for you as a friend and see your crazy Uncle Earl," said the jubilant Hope.

"What a surprise, and how nice of you. Hey, would you like to meet for breakfast when I get off in the morning, if it's not too early for you?" Divine asked, anxious to see her again.

"State the time and place, and I'll be there."

After Divine told her where the meeting spot would be and what time to meet him there, he proceeded with his job, working diligently so he would be able to leave on time.

Hope arrived at the diner in casual attire, wearing grey shorts, a pink half shirt that was tied in the front and showed off her flat stomach, matching tennis shoes with the pink ball on the back of her white socks, and a pink baseball cap with a white logo on it.

Over breakfast, Hope announced that there was a possibility she would be moving back to Atlanta soon.

"I want to start over and do things the way I'm supposed to. It seems like a few job opportunities that I've applied for might come through for me," Hope said.

"It would certainly be nice to have you closer. I really needed this conversation to keep from going insane," added Divine, while grinning. "I often wonder why my wife can't have a few of your characteristics. It seems like Destiny and I just aren't on the same level, and I'm tired of trying to pull teeth to get her to see my vision."

"She may have personal issues, but she definitely has one characteristic of finding a way to a man's heart because home girl is feeding you. Divine, you have gained a little weight since the last time I've seen you," laughed Hope.

"Yeah, she loves to cook, which is good for a grown man like me," responded Divine.

"Yeah, and her ass is probably putting little extra sprinkles and spices in your food, too, that's going to have you flipping out in a minute," Hope teased, as Divine laughed.

"Don't say that because she can really throw down in the kitchen. Now you got me thinking about that mess," chuckled Divine.

"Shit, I personally think some people are just stupid and would do anything to get a man or a woman. Some people will let their partner dog them out and put up with crap just to say I have a man. Some will settle just to screw someone to get a credit card, and others will just have low self-esteem in order to just be loved. I really don't understand the whole love thing, but I know it's a bitch and could have someone going crazy if it's not looked at from the right angle that God is love," said Hope.

"High school sweetheart, you said a mouth full," Divine replied, as his phone rang. He looked at his caller ID to see Cherish's number on the display. "What's up, cuz?"

"Daddy has died," wept Cherish uncontrollably.

"I'll be right there," Divine quickly said, before hanging up and looking at Hope to deliver the news.

"It's going to be okay, Divine," Hope said, then rose to go to the other side of the table to hug and console him in his time of need.

CHAPTER 28

"Hey, are you okay and have everything squared away for tomorrow?" asked Hope, who left the day before the funeral to return to the Constitution State.

"I'm fine, sweetie. Thanks for being there for me."

"Don't mention it," Hope replied. "Just call if you need anything."

Why can't my wife be attentive like Hope, he thought while ending the call.

The morning of the funeral, Destiny sent a text to Faith to inform her that she was going with Divine to his uncle's funeral.

Destiny, you do know that if you go, you're going to have to answer all kinds of questions from Divine's phony folks about where you've been and be confronted by the controversial stories regarding your marital problems, responded Faith in her text. *Why don't you just come chill with me at the hotel off Peachtree? We can do a movie and drinks later so you won't get yourself into a situation you would rather not find yourself in,* suggested Faith, sending multiple texts.

The truth of the matter was Faith was more concerned about the possibility that Destiny and Divine would reconcile than she was with the possibility of Destiny being interrogated by Divine's family.

After thinking about what Faith had texted her, Destiny placed a call to Divine and used the excuse of not being able to take time off of work. He was not happy to say the least; however, he understood the position she was in with having to choose between her job and attending the funeral.

However, while driving down Peachtree on his way to the funeral, he spotted Destiny's car parked in the lot of a nearby hotel.

What the fuck, he thought as he quickly pulled into the lot, got out of his car, and advanced to Destiny's car to look through the tinted windows at Desire's car seat and Destiny's personal belongings in the backseat. After trying to call Destiny several times, but not getting an answer because her phone was turned off, he went inside to ask the clerk if she had seen a dark-skinned lady come through the lobby.

"No, I haven't," replied the clerk, as Divine stood pissed.

"My wife has to be here because her car is outside," Divine explained before asking her to check her hotel guest list for anyone staying there under Destiny's married or maiden last names.

"No, sir, I'm afraid not," replied the young lady after looking through the hotel's computer guest list. "Would you like for me to search under a different last name?"

"Never mind," Divine told her, knowing he couldn't waste anymore time trying to hunt Destiny down because he would end up being late for his uncle's funeral if he did.

Later that day, Destiny called Divine to check on him.

"Please don't act concerned now. You have done nothing but reject, embarrass, and disrespect me throughout this entire marriage," Divine spat.

"I guess you don't want to talk," said Destiny, as her conscience played on her.

"About what?" shouted the wounded Divine.

"Look, Divine, I'm not going to sit on the phone and fight with you," Destiny replied.

"I am mentally hurt, miserable, and thinking the worse about this marriage because you're not hearing or feeling me. I saw your car somewhere today where I didn't need to see it, and before you can fix your lips to form some lie, we really need to call Pastor now and get counseling," said Divine, being straightforward.

"Look, I don't know what you're talking about by my car being somewhere. They make more than one make, year, and model of a car. And as far as counseling goes, I've told you my view on that. So, I guess on this two-party conversation between me and you, I'm asking for you to agree with me on the divorce because we need to do this so I can be straight before it's time for me to file my income taxes," replied Destiny, using her attitude and self-centeredness to cover her guilt.

This girl really does have split personalities, Divine thought, then said, "Look, Destiny, I'm glad you're taking this whole ordeal as a fucking game."

"Excuse me?" replied Destiny, frowned up her face on the other end of the phone.

"Look, you're right. We don't need to talk to no one. And just to let you know, I'm going to do what I have to do to prove to you that I'm not playing a mutherfucking game with you?" said Divine, then hung the phone up on Destiny.

"How's my buddy doing?" asked Hope, contacting Divine a few days later.

"I'm alright. I'm just at the house feeling mentally damaged and abused. It's to the point where I don't even want to love again after this divorce. If I didn't know you from childhood and know that there are a few good women left out there, I don't think I would be able to love and to do the whole marriage thing again. It's just too much," replied the exhausted Divine.

"Awww, it will work out for you, D. Hold your head up, boy. Don't let your past be in the driver seat of your future. I've been bad mouthed and walked through the shadow of death, but I come to tell you right now that my day is fine and my future ahead is going to be tremendous because I'm back on the market. How about my loser roommate has gone to jail for robbing a store and shooting the clerk in the shoulder. He keeps calling here crying and asking me to bail him out. I only accepted one collect call from him, and when I did, I told him 'No. Thanks for everything, and God bless.'"

"Hold on…hold on. Wait…wait! Girl, that's too much stuff that's been happening," Divine said, shocked to hear that Hope's relationship had finally come to an end.

"Divine, after all the years I've invested in this relationship, been faithful to him, and put up with his bull, how about some girl called me saying that she had his phone and was going through it to call all the girl's numbers and ask that they don't call him anymore. When I asked the girl who she might be, she said, 'I'm his girlfriend of three years'. D, I almost flipped out of a damn oak tree when I heard that shit. Boy, I just didn't know how to react. I wanted to kill that boy myself, but thank God he was already locked up when I found out. I've learned that you can't help anyone that doesn't want to help themselves. So, I'm presently waiting for something to come through from the job applications I have submitted in Atlanta. I may be your neighbor sooner than you think."

"And I will be more than happy to welcome you into the neighborhood. Hell, I'll even bring you over a pie," Divine replied.

After hanging up, he glowed on the inside over the fact that Hope would soon be closer to him.

The next morning, Divine went to pick up Uncle Earl's wife to take her to the lawyer's office downtown.

"Baby, are we still in Atlanta?" asked the seasoned woman, while looking up at the tall buildings.

"Yes, auntie," Divine replied, as he laughed.

"It's been a while since I've come downtown, seeing all these new high rises," she said in awe, seeing such change over time with the growth of the city.

"Yeah, I guess this part of city has changed a little bit since you have come down here."

"So are you still married?" she questioned, wanting the 411 on Divine's relationship.

"Yes, ma'am, for right now I am. I'm still praying and fasting over my marriage, and I need to talk to the pastor again before I file for the divorce," replied Divine in shame.

"Well, before you handpick another woman to be your wife out of desperation, make sure it last longer than a revolution. Now, that doesn't mean you have to settle, but just make sure you last long enough to cut the frozen first piece of cake that represents the one year anniversary. Heck, you young people dun had me get all dressed up for something that didn't even last a few months," Uncle Earl's wife said, as Divine just shook his head and listened.

After the lawyer met with Uncle Earl's wife, Danny Boy, Cherish, and Divine, he explained in detail what assets were left to Cherish and Danny Boy, who were happy with the many rental properties that Uncle Earl owned. He then turned to Divine and announced that Uncle Earl had left him his half-million dollar cleaning business. Instantly, Divine began to cry and sent up 'Thank you, Jesus' praises. That night, he went by the church and dropped a thank-you note to Jesus in the box located in the church's foyer.

CHAPTER 29

"Wow, I'm back. It feels like I haven't seen you in ages, and it's only been a month or so ago," said Hope, who had landed a job as a loan officer and moved back to Atlanta.

"Can you give us a few minutes?" Divine asked the waiter.

"Certainly, sir. Take your time."

The two looked at the menu of the Italian restaurant strangely, not knowing what to order, but not wanting to feel dumb by saying anything.

"Would you like to try our special for today?" asked the waiter, returning a short while later with his pad and pencil in hand.

Divine knew that was his moment to say something to get the pressure off him by saying something dumb. "Hell, Hope, just say yeah because you can't pronounce a thing on the menu," teased Divine, as Hope burst out laughing.

"Boy, you crazy. You're the one who can't pronounce anything," replied Hope, as she told the waiter to let Divine order first because she was still looking, putting Divine on the spot.

"Whatever! Excuse me, waiter, do you have anything with a little bit of added spices on some type of chicken? I need something that's scrumptious and yummy for my tummy right about now," Divine said.

"Why yes we do, there's a heavenly dish that comes with two sides right here" replied the waiter as Divine looked at Hope and winked his eye as she shot him a bird as she held her menu.

"And you, ma'am?" asked the waiter.

"Well, sir, I may have to order for her," laughed Divine, as Hope pointed to the featured ambrosial food displayed in a picture to place her order.

As the two began to talk while waiting on their food, Hope told Divine about her new job.

"Everything seems like it was all set up for me to come back home because I applied for this same position a while ago with this company and they didn't call me back until now. I feel so blessed to be in this position right now. I just have to get back to the busy city life and adjust to a few new people at my job. But I'll be fine with that because I'm happy to be back home," smiled Hope.

"Well, I'm happy that you're back. I've been praying for days like this just to chill and hangout," replied Divine, being appreciative of their outing. "What possessed you to move away with a drug dealer anyway?"

"You know, I was just looking at the easiest route I could take to gain success. I was ready for something new and took advantage of my opportunity with my boyfriend who had money. But, as I settled in and saw things change with him going to jail and no money coming in, it caused me to grow up and do things on my own. It also taught me that everything that glitters ain't gold," Hope shared.

"Tell me about it. I can certainly vouch for that. I can speak from my marriage that some of those who seem 'well put together' soon unravel at the seams," commented Divine, as the waiter sat their food down in front of them.

"So, what do you think would be up with us if you ever heal from your divorce? What exactly would you be looking for in a mate the next time?" asked Hope, as they ate.

"Well, since I think I got married too soon and for the wrong reasons, I'll play it by ear with our friendship and would like for us to get to know each other more, such as learning about our credit history, debts owed, family background, and all the other small stuff in order to avoid major problems later on down the road. Of course, I know that with as beautiful and sexy as you are, I may slip a few times with the premarital sex and have to ask God to forgive me," teased Divine.

"Alright now, God's gonna get tired of you repenting for the same thing," Hope replied, letting him know that he couldn't keep doing the same old tricks after being saved.

"Well, no sin is greater than the next, and I do serve a forgiving God. He'll deliver me in due season if I try to make efforts to stop."

"Amen," Hope replied, as they enjoyed the rest of their dinner and evening together.

That Sunday, Divine invited Hope to join him at church. As Divine and Hope sat next to Cherish, Danny Boy, and his wife, Destiny, who was singing in the choir, noticed Divine, who hadn't called her in a few days begging her to return home, was sitting next to a pretty woman.

After the service, Destiny darted towards the group with envy in her eyes. As she approached them, she grabbed Divine's right arm, causing him to spin around to face her as she looked him dead in the eyes.

"Divine, what are you doing?" shouted Destiny in a stern voice, her eyebrows furrowed.

"I'm not doing anything," replied Divine in an innocent and nonchalant voice.

"Who is this?" questioned Destiny with an attitude.

"Hope," replied Divine, who had nothing to hide.

"Oh, heck naw! You mean to tell me you brought the girl whose name you have called me before to our church!" yelled Destiny, while cutting her eyes at Hope.

"Calm down," whispered Divine, in an attempt to have her lower her voice while inside the house of the Lord.

"Screw what you're saying right now," said Destiny, as she pushed Divine aside and stepped closer towards Hope. "Do you know you're with a married man?" Destiny asked in a nasty tone.

"I'm not in that. That's between you guys," responded Hope, while trying to maintain her cool.

"You are in it because you're with *my* husband in *my* church," explained Destiny, while raising her voice and inching closer.

"Don't be yelling at my friend, Destiny," said Divine, as he raised his voice to draw the line between the outrage.

"You're right, Divine. Your wife shouldn't be arguing with me, because she doesn't know me like that," Hope replied, sending a warning to Destiny.

"You know what, Divine? I got something for you!" shouted Destiny, as she slapped Divine hard across the face and then quickly walked off to join her friends who were watching nearby.

"Are you okay?" asked Hope with concern.

"Yes, but that was the final straw," Divine said, as they left church and went to the police station to file a restraining order against Destiny.

After receiving the restraining order, Destiny took her chances of violating the order by calling Divine to apologize for her actions.

"I'm sorry about hitting you in church, but I was so mad to see you with someone else," said Destiny remorsefully.

"I accept your apology, but I'm still going to go through with the divorce. You know, Destiny, I love you with every inch of me, but I've come to accept that love is just not enough," he replied before ending the call.

CHAPTER 30

As the mediation day came, Divine stood on the back patio of Hope's house and stared out at the beautiful lakeside view, as the birds flew over their heads and the sun beamed down upon them.

"I sure don't feel like going in here today to defend myself against all these false allegations Destiny has said about me. I hope I don't have to go into depth about Uncle Earl's business that she's trying to get half of," said Divine, and then exhaled.

"Just make sure you read all the papers and confirm the things you have and don't have. You'll be okay. Just don't be all shy and fuzzy. At least it will be over within a few months and you'll be stress free," smiled Hope, as the slight breeze blew the branches of the trees back and forth.

"Yeah, I hope. I know I need to be just as careful getting out of this mess as I was getting in."

"Let's join hands and pray about it," Hope said, leading Divine in a brief prayer.

"Alright, I'll call and let you know how things turn out," he said before leaving the house.

After Destiny and Divine arrived at the courthouse to pay their paperwork fee, the mediator met with the two as she read off all the things that Destiny requested on her list.

This is going to be ugly, Divine thought. *Lord, just tell me what to say. Please speak through me on how to respond in this situation I've never been in before.*

As soon as the mediator finished reading Divine's few items, Destiny saw that Divine wasn't trying to get anything from her. So, while looking at the mediator, she changed her request. "Just disregard all of my valuables and assets I said I want in the letter."

Divine looked at Destiny with a surprised looked.

"Are you sure? You have some expensive items down here," asked the mediator, not understanding her decision.

"Yeah, just forget them. The next relationship I get into I'm going to start from scratch and let the man be the head provider like he should," Destiny replied, delivering a low blow below the belt, as Divine just shook his head at her comment.

Without any further questioning, the mediator had them sign the necessary papers and then informed them on their wait time for their court date.

A few months passed with Destiny and Divine's divorce day coming during the summer time. Divine sat in the hallway waiting to be called into the divorce room, as Destiny sat across from him with a depressed look on her face.

"So this is it? The end of Double D," Destiny said in a downcast tone.

"I still love you and Desire to this day, and if you decided to move on with someone else, I'll still love you the same. Scars heal and fade, but memories don't all the time. You just have to have a forgiving heart like God when someone does you wrong," responded Divine.

"Yeah, you're right. I fear the thought of getting with someone else who I don't know. I've been dating this one person, but I don't know what's up with it."

"Well, just take every learning experience that you've had in this marriage and your past relationships into the new one," Divine suggested.

As the officer called the two to enter the room, Destiny asked, "Why exactly did you leave me?"

"I really just began to think about what if something ever happened to me. Would you be that woman to take care of me and clean me? Would you be the woman to stay true to the vow to death do us part? I just had that unstable confirmation that you wouldn't guarantee that by your actions as my wife," replied Divine, as they walked in the courtroom and took seats across from each other at the table.

After being sworn in to answer a few questions and agreeing to the mediation review in front of the judge, the divorce was final and

Destiny and Divine were officially free from each other.

When Divine walked out the room, with Destiny following a few steps behind him, he looked up to see Faith standing in the courtroom lobby staring at him.

What the fuck, thought Divine, while Faith started walking towards him.

"Hey, Divine," smiled Faith, as she waved the two-karat tennis bracelet on her wrist that Destiny had charged on Divine's jewelry account for her. "I'm glad some casinos payoff very well." Then she walked past Divine to start hugging and tongue kissing Destiny in the lobby.

Divine stood in shock looking at them make out in the courtroom lobby in front of everyone.

As Divine looked at the two, not believing what was going on before his very eyes, little signs started to be revealed to him, such as the tattoo of Misty's name on Faith's back and Destiny yelling out Big Daddy during sex with him.

"Y'all are some sick individuals. Peace!" Divine shouted as he quickly left the courthouse to return home, where he sat in awe on the couch, not telling Hope what happened.

Hope sensed the maybe something had happened at the divorce proceedings, but she didn't prod by asking questions. Instead, she wanted to take Divine's mind off the happenings of the day.

"Lay down, baby, and relax," Hope told him.

As she walked off to get the tweezers, a towel, and face cleanser, Divine's phone started to ring non-stop with calls from Destiny, which he ignored. They were now divorced with no strings attached. So, there is no reason she should have been calling. Therefore, he decided not to even entertain her by answering.

"I got you, baby," said Hope, as she began to clean Divine's face, while he stared up at the ceiling in a daze and replayed what had started with a one-night stand with Faith and led to him getting married and divorced from Destiny.

After pulling out some ingrown hairs on Divine's face that had caused a few pimples, Hope became irritated with Destiny insistently calling.

"I don't mean to be rude, Divine, and answer your shit, but if that bitch calls your phone one more time, she's going to get told the business for disrespecting mine," Hope said, growing irritated.

No sooner had the words left her mouth his phone rang yet again.

"Look, Destiny, if you don't stop calling Divine, there's going to be problems," Hope threatened, answering his phone. "You're crying now over something you had and lost. You've mistreated instead of loved, and now you miss what you threw to the wolves. Don't be crying to have back now what's my silver and gold in heaven. Now stop calling here before I beat your ass like a candy-filled piñata. And you can go get whoever so I can pass out the candy because there's enough to go around forever and anyone," said Hope, reading Destiny and then hanging up on her before she could get one word out her mouth.

After that, Destiny never called back and she even stopped going to the same church as Hope and Divine.

Divine soon extended his relationship with his roommate, as they dated seriously without worrying about a label.

"D, I really missed you when I was away," Hope expressed, opening up to him.

"I missed you, too. Why don't you let me show you how much?"

After Divine blessed Hope's beautiful body with a baby oil bath, which caused her skin to have rose petal softness, he began to kiss on her. His tongue wandered all over her body until it found the circle of hope, as his tongue played with the ring for hours like a little kid eating cotton candy at the fair.

Two years later, Hope sold her townhome in Atlanta and moved with her husband Divine to Charlotte, North Carolina, where his half million dollar Divine Shine business had expanded. The now pregnant real estate consultant Hope was approached by a new co-worker who told her that she looked familiar. Although Hope was not sure where she knew her from, the two vibed well and became associates, often going on their lunch breaks together.

After receiving countless 'don't block your blessing' gifts from the woman, Hope told her that she was due to have her baby any day, as the woman replied, "Just let me know and I'll bring a special gift basket for you and your family."

A few days later, Hope had to go to the hospital to have her labor induced. Divine sat by the side of her bed all day watching the monitor, as the top line showed the heart rate and the bottom line showed the intensity and frequency of the contractions.

As the day progressed and the contractions went from being ten minutes apart to two minutes, her cervix was almost at ten centimeters. Hope felt uncomfortable and suddenly felt the urge to push whenever the contractions hit her.

"Divine, get the doctor!" yelled Hope, as she started to scream in pain.

As the doctor rushed in the room, he told Divine, "Sir, you better brace yourself because we're getting ready to have this baby," then called for the nurses to help assist in the delivery of Divine and Hope's first child, while Divine took pictures.

"Well, tongue, you'll never taste that again after seeing this freaked out stuff," giggled Divine, as he shared the pictures from the birth of their daughter with Hope.

"Shut up, crazy," smiled Hope, while looking at the camera's display screen.

Just then, her hospital phone rang and she handed the camera back to Divine so she could answer it, thinking it was some more family members calling to congratulate them.

"I'm fine," Hope said upon answering the phone. "Okay, girl, I'll tell Divine to help you bring the flowers and gifts up to the room. Hold on while I ask him. Baby," she said, addressing Divine, "can you go downstairs and help my friend up to the room with the gifts out of her car? She said she has too much to carry in one trip, and I don't want to make her have to go back and forth."

"Sure, baby," he replied, as he took the phone so he could talk with his wife's friend.

"Where actually are you?" Divine asked, as the woman with the deep voice told him that she was downstairs in the south parking lot.

After Divine got downstairs and walked through the parking lot while humming a song of joy, he approached the 760 BMW that had tinted windows and was sitting on 22-inch tires.

When he knocked on the window and the driver lowered it, he couldn't believe his eyes.

"Hey, Divine," Faith said, while staring back at him with a sinister smile.

THE END?

GROUP DISCUSSION QUESTIONS

1. Can one give too much or not enough in a relationship? What signs are present when one partner is giving more than the other? Was Divine a good husband to Destiny?

2. What makes a man/woman commit to one lover opposed to another?

3. Was Neal a true friend to Divine? Do you find this type of deception more common in male/male relationships or female/female relationships?

4. Should Hope have continued with her relationship with her two-timing, dope-dealing boyfriend? Do you believe she stayed with her boyfriend out of fear or obligation?

5. Did Divine, Hope, Faith, or Destiny truly understand the meaning of love? Did either of them love themselves?

6. What are your feelings on Destiny and Divine's intimate relationship as Christians? Is it right for believers to live together prior to marriage?

7. Was Hope sincere about wanting Destiny and Divine's marriage to work? Was she being a friend when she flew to Atlanta when Divine's uncle was ill, or was she capitalizing on an opportunity to win Divine's heart?

8. As a wife or husband, would you allow the other spouse total control over the finances? Was Destiny being totally unreasonable when Divine was trying to make a better way for his family?

9. Do all friendships with someone of the opposite sex have to end when marriage is introduced into an intimate relationship?

10. Why is it difficult for a man to tell a new female in his life what he really wants from her? Why do women feel as though they can change a man's mind about what he wants from her? By him not

telling her what he really wants from her, is that leading her on? By the woman thinking she can change his mind, is she setting herself up for hurt and disappointment?

11. Why do some individuals hide behind spirituality to mask who they really are? Who do you feel was masking: Hope, Destiny or Divine? Do you believe Divine's transformation from playa to saint was sincere?

12. Do you believe Destiny was intoxicated when she had sex with Faith? Was both Destiny and Divine so intoxicated that they did not detect Faith in their bedroom having her way with both of them?

13. Do you believe Faith to be a mental case or a master manipulator? What could Divine have done differently concerning Faith?

14. With Faith lurking in the wings, do you believe Divine and Hope have a solid future ahead of them? Why or why not?